Praise for Kim Rees' *Buying Mackenzie's Baby*

5 Hearts "Ms. Kim Rees did a wonderful job of telling this story. It was certainly not boring! With so many characters, it would seem that the story would be confusing, but that definitely was not the case. She told the story so well that I (the reader) felt I was living in the situation and could not help, even though I wanted to. I would recommend this book to anyone who likes to read romance; there will definitely be no disappointment!"

~ *Brenda Talley, The Romance Studio*

4.5 Blue Ribbons "This gripping novel is choked full of turbulent emotions and hidden agendas. Kim has me praying that Kate and Mack do not destroy each other and the love they have within their grasp with their misconceptions of each other and the unwelcome interference of malicious bystanders. Definitely an unforgettable masterpiece by the incomparable Kim Rees."

~ *JT, Romance Junkies*

4 Angels "**Kim Rees** has penned an overwhelming emotional story. Romance fans who love a lot of angst, intensity, and pent-up emotions will become happily engrossed in *Buying Mackenzie's Baby*."

~ *Sarah W, Fallen Angel Reviews*

Buying Mackenzie's Baby

Kim Rees

A SAMHAIN PUBLISHING, LTD. publication.

Samhain Publishing, Ltd.
2932 Ross Clark Circle, #384
Dothan, AL 36301
www.samhainpublishing.com

Buying Mackenzie's Baby
Copyright © 2006 by Kim Rees
Print ISBN: 1-59998-382-6
Digital ISBN: 1-59998-025-8

Editing by Sasha Knight
Cover by Scott Carpenter

First Samhain Publishing, Ltd. electronic publication: September 2006
First Samhain Publishing, Ltd. print publication: December 2006

Dedication

To Georgie, Ed, Daniel and Jack…for putting up with me!

Prologue

"Note to self. Don't drink vodka. Again. Ever."

Kate rubbed at sticky eyes and dragged at her face with tight fingers. Her head pounded. She stared up at the white ceiling.

Something was wrong. She blinked. It was silly, ridiculous, but the ceiling seemed to be a lot further away. Her bedroom ceiling was low, had a damp patch and swirly patterns. Definitely not high and edged with intricate geometric moulding.

"Okay, still dreaming."

Her hazy mind happy, she yawned, stretching her spine against the smoothness of the sheets. And froze. Sensation bombarded her. The light scent of lavender. A mattress that didn't squeal and squeak with every movement. The soft weight of blankets, when she had a heavy duvet, and a sleek warmth to the sheets that caressed her very naked skin. Naked. She didn't sleep naked. Couldn't. It was too cold, what with the old heating.

Kate pulled in her scattering thoughts. Her heart hammered, eclipsing the pounding in her head. She remembered to breathe. "All right. Don't panic." She tried not to hear the fear in her own voice. "I'm in a strange bed and I'm naked. That doesn't necessarily mean—"

Her attention shot to her right as the mattress shifted. Rich, woolen blankets slipped. Horror tightened her already nervous stomach and blood rushed into her face. A man's tousled, sandy hair. Her gaze snapped away and fixed on the high ceiling. She had to get—

More movement. A heavy arm fell across her and Kate's teeth dug at her lip, biting back the yelp. Too late. Too late to make an anonymous escape.

Her hands clenched. Maybe if she eased out of the bed, let that warm, strong arm slip, slide over her body...

Kate gasped. Memories of a touch, the fiery stroke of impatient fingers, a mouth sliding hot and wet over her skin. Arching under the weight of another body. The ecstasy of skin against skin. Oh God. She had...

With a complete stranger.

Her mind shot into the present. The stranger shifted. A large, warm hand splayed over her stomach and those clever fingers started to move. A gentle, almost sleepy caress sparked flickers of fire under her skin. How? This didn't happen to her. Hadn't since...him.

Kate closed her eyes, not wanting to deny the curl of heat low in her belly. Only Mack had ever made her skin burn. "Not him. Not now." Finally, after years of misery, she could put the pain of that man behind her.

"Hmm?"

Even muffled by the blankets, the soft, deep voice made her toes curl. That and what his equally clever mouth—

"Nothing," Kate gasped.

"Like that?"

"God, yes."

"And this?"

Kate became lost in her own rapid breathing. An involuntary little squeal escaped her. But then— "Don't stop. Oh God, please, don't stop."

Blankets ripped back with a string of expletives. His eyes. Their burning anger slashed across her face and Kate flinched against it. All desire shriveled. Something sick lurched in her stomach. Not a stranger. Kate's eyes crushed shut, blocking out the cold hatred in his dark brown gaze. She fought back the sting of tears, her hands covering her scalding face. "No!" It was almost a wail.

Cold air washed over her skin. He snatched up the top sheet and Kate made a sudden scramble for anything to cover her nakedness.

"What a pleasant surprise to see you too, Kate."

Her hangover burst back. She groaned. Unthinking, she stared at his naked torso, delaying on his arms. His smooth brown skin, still with beautifully sharp muscle definition. She had always loved—

No, not going there. This man had torn out her heart and stamped on it. "What the hell are you doing in my bed?" Good. Anger. Much better than the other feeling.

"*Your* bed?" He was on his feet, fingers bunching the white sheet around his waist. His hard glare swept over the clean, pale walls and then fixed on her. Steel bands contracted around her chest at the derision she found there. "Since when could *you* afford a room like this?" His voice grated and dark eyes narrowed. "Did you do this hoping for a handout?"

The blood burned in her face. Money. It always came back to money with Sean Mackenzie. A wife was only a drain. It was why she hadn't taken a penny from him when they divorced. Her arms tightened convulsively around the blanket covering her breasts. Not a penny. "You haven't changed, Mack."

"Where you're concerned? No. Never. Now get out."

"Then turn around."

A bark of harsh laughter made her jump. "You have nothing I want to see."

"That wasn't the impression you just gave."

He smirked, and the callous glitter sharpened his eyes. "A naked woman in my bed? Offering herself?" Mack's voice was a caress and Kate fought the shiver rippling over her skin. Fought and lost. "What's a man to do?"

He could never resist. No, not going to that memory she had of Angela. "Yes. I see."

Kate pulled in her courage and swung her legs over the edge of the bed. Her toes dug into the deep softness of the rug. Mack's gaze prickled over her as she shuffled across the room. Clothes, underwear, both hers and his, were flung around the room. Her face reddened. Awkwardly, she pulled on her underwear, shrugged into her crumpled dress and tried desperately to keep as much of her body covered with the light blanket.

Mack, relaxing on the bed, his long, lean body barely covered by that white sheet, a cruel smile cutting his mouth, was obviously enjoying her struggle. "How was it for you, Kate?"

She watched her hands rub down the creases of her silver, sheath dress, preparing her face for the lie. "Not very memorable, Mack." She looked up and gave him a sharp smile. "Sorry."

"So you didn't scream my name?" He picked at a piece of fluff on the sheet. "Beg me to take you again?" An eyebrow rose. "And again?" His smile was to himself. "Maybe your acting *is* worth payment. My wallet's on the dresser. Take what's there."

Kate stared. Fury had her shaking. For one moment, she'd thought he was another man, one who had broken Mack's spell over her body. But no. Stupidly, she'd had sex with Sean Mackenzie. And he hadn't changed. "No," she grated. "And it'll be a cold day in hell before I touch it, or you, ever again."

Hot, angry tears blurred her eyes as she ran from his hotel room.

Chapter One

Kate Hartley stared up at the towering office block, steel and glass dazzling in the early morning sunshine. Her palms were sweating and she rubbed them on the smooth material of her skirt. She winced as the skirt shifted. She plucked it back into place. Two months ago, it had been a perfect fit. Two months. She took a deep breath and started up the wide, granite steps.

People rushed past her, eager to start the working day. Kate was far from eager. If she could only stretch time. She ran a trembling hand over her hair, feeling the cool smoothness. All right. She could do this. She blew out a slow breath. Of course, she had *no* choice.

She straightened her spine and trotted up the last three steps that led to the entrance.

Kate made the mistake of catching her reflection in the shining glass door. That stopped her. A woman of average height, in a dark blue suit that swam on her. Black hair scraped back from a gaunt face. Her skin was grey, really grey, in the fresh sunlight. And her eyes. Dark circled, dulled to murky blue. She had never been pretty, but now she looked a complete mess.

The thought of how he would look at her made her stomach knot. "Tough," she muttered and stepped forward, watching the glass slide away.

Her low heels clicked over the marble flooring. The sharp scent of lemon polish itched at her nostrils and she tried to take her mind off it by staring around the airy, open space. Gleaming steel lifts, men and women in expensive suits, burdened with briefcases and laptop bags, waiting impatiently, all eyes fixed on the floor indicators. A solid teak, circular reception desk set in the center of the entrance area. It caught the long shafts of golden light streaming in from the glass façade. Deep, cream sofas and large exotic plants surrounded the reception. The continual ringing of the telephones and the clamor of voices did little to ease Kate's nerves.

She waited while one of the tall, beautifully plastic receptionists finished her telephone conversation. The lump of misery sat heavy in Kate's uneasy stomach. She knew how dreadful she looked.

Kate blinked. The receptionist was subjecting her to a toothy smile.

"Welcome to Mackenzie International. How may I help you?"

Bright, perky and beautiful at eight in the morning. Kate hated her. "Hello." She swallowed back her nervousness. "I'm Dr. Catherine Hartley. I'd like to see Sean Mackenzie please."

"Have you an appointment?"

"No. Could you tell him I'm here?"

The smile widened. And still that oh-so-pleasant voice. A perfect, plastic wall. "Dr. Hartley, you must understand, Mr. Mackenzie is a very busy man. I can contact his PA, have her arrange—"

God, not her. The panicked thought shot through Kate's brain. The words were out before she realized it. "I'm his ex-wife." Something flickered in the plastic façade. Great. What was the rumor about her now? Seven years before, it had been Sean Mackenzie's folly. His child-bride, only nineteen. "Could you call him, please?"

"If you would like to take a seat please, Dr. Hartley?" The receptionist waved an expertly manicured hand to the cluster of sofas.

Kate sighed and headed reluctantly to the nearest sofa. Her body sank into the soft leather. She bit at her lip, trying not to breathe in the material's thick odor. To distract her, Kate concentrated on the receptionist's smooth features. Watched as she turned slightly, obviously sharing new gossip about the state of the boss's ex-wife.

"No choice in this," she murmured, feeling the sting of tears. "None."

Damn it, she would not cry. Mack would know he was her last resort. She'd had a job for the summer, tiding her over until term started again. Francesca had been counting on her, counting on the money to support her. But the job had been impossible. Her sister had swallowed what little savings Kate had and now her mortgage had fallen into arrears. If it was only herself, Kate could've coped, she would have put her flat up for sale and slept on a friend's floor.

But her condition had made her delay even that desperate measure and now selling was impossible too. The letter sat on her hall table. The bank had started repossession proceedings the day before. It was why she was sitting there, waiting to know if Sean Mackenzie would deign to see her. No money. No home. That alone would not have brought her to him, begging for a handout. The word shriveled her insides. But it wasn't just her. She stared down at her still flat stomach. Not anymore.

"Dr. Hartley?"

Her attention snapped to the woman. She pushed herself up and tried to smile. Kate ran her fingers over her rumpled jacket and wished that her heart wasn't lodged in her throat. What if he said no? What she had to say, to ask for, had to be done face to face. She was dreading it

"Mr. Mackenzie's assistant will be with you shortly."

Finally, the words broke through her panic. Did that mean...? Wait. His assistant? "Angela Craven?" She bit out the name.

"Yes."

Kate remembered to be polite. "Thank you for your help." She waved back to the sofas. "I'll be over there."

Anger burned in her gut. Angela Craven. After seven years had passed, she shouldn't be bitter. Her marriage to Mack had been an aberration, a brief summer fling. He then returned to the real woman in his life, his very *personal* assistant. One past image seared into her brain. Standing in the doorway of Mack's office, watching them, listening to them—

"Kate. Hello."

Her smooth liquid voice. Kate opened her eyes and made a smile work across her mouth. Angela had to be in her early thirties now. Tall, immaculately dressed, her glossy, chestnut hair loosely piled on her head. Angela's fine, lightly tanned skin shone with health. Kate resisted the urge to touch her own face, aware that her skin was sallow in comparison. She met eyes as dark as Mack's and withered under the falsely pleasant smile. Kate remembered it well. "Angela." She found her unsteady feet, driving down her dislike of the woman. She had more important things to worry about. "Will Mack see me?"

"He said I was to bring you straight up."

Kate couldn't help the relieved sigh. "Good. Thank you."

"What brings you back here, after what, seven years?"

Kate concentrated on walking to the lifts, placing one foot in front of the other. Angela walked beside her, heels clacking over the marble. Her perfume smelled like over-sweet, thick toffee, cloying, lodging at the back of Kate's throat. She stared at their reflections caught in the lift doors, trying not to see the golden glow that was Angela Craven. Her fingers pressed to her lips. Mack's office was on the thirtieth floor. An age in an enclosed box with that perfume.

Belatedly, Kate remembered that Angela had been talking to her. "Sorry, what did you say?"

Now there was a slight hint of steel in her voice. "Why are you here, Kate?"

The lift pinged and the wide doors slid silently open. Kate stepped inside and leaned back against the rail. Her gaze fixed on the floor, on the tufts of dark blue carpeting. The door closed and she was trapped with Angela's overpowering scent. She gripped the cold metal rail with clammy hands. Her stomach wanted to revolt. "I was passing," she murmured. "Thought I'd drop in."

"After all this time?"

"Yes."

"Mack has only agreed to five minutes."

"That's all I'll need."

The lift pinged again and she could finally step out into the fresher air of the open plan area. She took deep, calming breaths, following Angela through the cube farms to Mack's office. It was strange to be back. If she hadn't fought so hard for that summer job when she was nineteen, she would not be in the trouble she was in now. Fear tightened her already unsettled stomach. What if he said no?

"Mack?"

Kate blinked, trying to focus her thoughts. Her insides jumped, but Angela was only knocking on the wide door. Mack's PA slipped inside and closed the door. The rush of anger burned Kate's cheeks and faded. She was too scared, and frankly too tired, to remain mad at

Angela Craven. After their last meeting, she could keep Sean Mackenzie.

Kate wiped a hand over her damp forehead. It was still too early for her to be up, but she knew Mack was always in his office first thing. And she wanted to get it over with.

The door swung back, making her jump. "Please come in, Dr. Hartley."

Kate stared at Angela, wondering at the sudden formality. "Yes." She stepped around the woman, trying not to breathe in her scent.

The familiar office. Walls of glass enclosed over half the room, offering stunning views of the city and the river, which glinted in the early morning sunshine. Sleek, pale furniture. His desk. Kate's fingers clenched as the memory of that dark night washed over her, seeing Angela wrapped around him, the thrust of his hips— Damn it, she would *not* cry. Sean Mackenzie had never loved her. It had been a wild burst of lust. That was all.

"Thank you, Angela."

Mack stood in the doorway to his private bathroom. A white towel hung around his neck and little flecks of shaving foam stained his cheeks. Her gaze slid down his bare chest, all too aware of the way the sunlight gleamed gold against his brown, muscled stomach.

"Do you want me to stay?"

Angela's voice, too close, jerked Kate's attention away. What was she doing? Starting a totally inappropriate examination of her very *ex-*husband? Color stained her cheeks and she stared down at the pale carpet.

"No, Angela. I'm sure I'll be quite safe."

Kate cringed at the words. He was mocking her. She pulled in her courage and lifted her eyes to his. Behind her, the door closed with a soft click. Her heart pounded in her ears. She wanted to blurt it out, get it over with. But Mack's cool expression tightened her throat.

His gaze slid from her with disdain. "Cold out?" He disappeared back into the bathroom.

"Excuse me?"

Mack reappeared, fastening buttons on a crisp, white shirt. He undid his belt and trousers to tuck in his shirt and Kate's eyes dropped again. Hazy, carnal images of the night in the hotel room swept over her. How he moved against her. Inside her. Kate flushed and her legs felt wobbly. It was because she was ill. It had nothing to do with the man in front of her. Nothing.

Mack looked up. His hatred killed her need. "Something like, I don't know, maybe a cold day in hell?"

Kate bit her lip. The memory of her furious words brought more heat to her face. She had meant them. Nothing would have brought her back. Nothing. But Fate had conspired. She rubbed a hand over her face. "May I sit down? Please?"

He waved at chairs set before the long stretch of windows. "Make yourself at home."

Mack was not making this easy. And when she told him... She fell into the chair and rested her spine against the soft back. The bag strap slipped from her shoulder. She remembered to take deep, calming breaths. Her gaze fell on the jug of ice water on the low table and with a shaking hand, Kate poured the water into a glass. It was a relief to let the cold, short sips slip down her tightened throat.

"So." Mack sat in a chair opposite to her, now also wearing a red tie and sharp, charcoal waistcoat. Kate blinked. He was equally beautiful dressed. "What do you want, Kate?"

Carefully, she placed her glass back on the small table. "This isn't easy, Mack."

"Asking for money never is. But you seem to have no trouble."

That's all she had ever been to him. Someone who took his precious cash. Kate let out a slow sigh, her attention fixed on the water jug. She wanted to explain the circumstances, not have him think he should support her because she was… It was still difficult even to think the word. "I had a job for the summer." She wished her voice sounded stronger, wished she could look into his face. But she was a coward.

"You? Working?"

That brought her head up, her pride stung. "I've worked since I was thirteen."

"Of course you have," Mack said, stretching his legs out and crossing them at the ankle. He waved a hand. "Continue with your tale of woe."

Kate wanted to slap him, slap him and storm out of his bloody office. She closed her eyes and blocked out the scorn on his sharp face. She didn't have that luxury. "I knew you'd be like this."

"Like what, Kate?" His harsh voice ripped her. "Not play along with your demands?"

She had to keep everything sensible, calm. She ignored his anger, plowing on. She watched her hands tighten into a bloodless knot in her lap. "As I was saying, I had a job. But then I found out— I got sick. It made working impossible."

"Sick?"

Kate wanted to think that it was worry in his voice, but his words dismissed the idea.

"What angle are you playing now? Expensive medical bills?"

"Will you let me finish?" Kate was on her feet, anger shaking her limbs. Too fast. Her stomach lurched. She clamped her hand to her mouth and ran for the bathroom. The door thumped shut and her fist slammed down on the lock. Mack would not see her like this.

After, Kate sank to the floor and let her head fall back against the beautifully cold tiles. She reached up to flush away her breakfast. She pulled a tissue from its holder and dabbed at her mouth, using another piece to wipe the tears from her eyes. Her throat was raw and her body would not stop trembling. "I hate throwing up."

The hammering finally broke through her daze. Kate sighed. Yes, she'd just vomited in Mack's executive toilet. He would not be pleased.

"Kate. What the hell is going on? Open this damn door!"

Reluctantly, she slid back up the wall. Her doctor had promised that her morning sickness would settle down in a few more weeks. "Easy for him to say." Kate stared at her flushed face, reddened eyes, disheveled hair. "Great. I look worse."

She took a deep breath, her hand delaying on the lock. Mack's scent wrapped around her, light, subtle. Kate rested her forehead briefly against the cool wood of the door, feeling Mack's fist pounding on the other side. He was the only man who had ever held her, held her and made her feel completely safe. Tears burned in her eyes, slipping again over her cheeks. It had been an illusion, a fantasy she had created. And then he'd tired of the naïve girl she had been.

She twisted the lock and pulled open the door.

"Kate." Unwilling, she met the hot anger in his gaze. She winced against the fingers biting into her upper arms. "Why lock the door?"

Kate shrugged off his fierce grip. She was numb in the face of his fury. It was stupid to hurt so much. Seven years. Worse was to know that inside her grew a tiny life, a part of the man she still— What? Wanted? Needed? Kate sighed. Now that would be stupid.

She found her abandoned glass and gulped down the rest of the water, wanting the raw taste in her mouth eased. "After I left your expensive hotel room, I wasn't thinking. I thought it would be all right." Her laugh was bitter. "No. Truthfully. I *really* wasn't thinking."

"Your point?"

She held his narrowed gaze and forced out the words. "I'm pregnant."

"Jesus, Kate, that was careless!"

She blinked. "Excuse me?"

He was pacing now. "You were looking for sex that night. Didn't you at least think to take *some* precautions?"

Her stomach knotted. He made her sound like a whore. "How dare you—"

"What do you want me to do?"

Kate would have loved to have told him that she was simply doing the honorable thing and keeping him informed. But that had never been an option. Her overdraft was strained to breaking and in a few days she wouldn't have anywhere to live. His reaction brought out bitter words. "Give me your money."

Fear washed over her as Mack stalked towards her, his face filled with fury. She shrank back into her seat, but couldn't resist when fierce hands dragged her up. "I will not pay for your abortion."

His words shot through her. She had never once thought of doing that. "I—"

"Or do you think this is your chance to get your claws into me again?" Mack's voice was cold, tight. The familiar burn in his eyes seared her. His fingers uncurled from her arms and she crumpled back into the softness of the chair.

How had she ever felt anything for the cruel, selfish man standing over her? "You think I want this? *Your* baby inside me?" She ignored the brief, unwanted tightening of her heart. She had once thought having their baby was her future.

"If it is mine."

Nothing was worth this. Nothing. She would scrounge somewhere to stay, sell her few possessions. Survive without him. Vainly, she still wished she had her wedding and engagement rings. But Mack, knowing their worth, had taken them back.

Kate leapt to her feet, her spine straight. "*You* were always the slut in this relationship, Mack." She took no delight in the shock that flashed across his harsh face. "I'll deal with this," she waved a hand at her flat stomach, "myself."

"I won't let you have an abortion."

"You can't dictate my life, Mack." Let him think what he liked. She and her baby would do very well without him. She lifted her chin and turned towards the door. "I'll be more than happy never to see you again."

A slow hand clap followed her footsteps. "You always do indignation so well." The sneer to his voice cut her. "Now, if you've finished with your theatrics?"

Anger twisted again in her gut. He had always thought this of her, thought her shallow. Kate stopped and turned, making herself hold his hard gaze. "What's there to discuss? You already doubt that the baby's yours."

"Yes, I do."

The bald statement stabbed at Kate, pricked tears at her eyes. She had promised herself she would do whatever was necessary to secure money from Mack. But this? She had never thought he would question her, practically accuse her of whoring around. Again.

"But you seem intent on burdening me with the responsibility. Therefore…" He straightened and waved at her chair. His eyes narrowed and Kate forced her slow, reluctant feet to take her back across the deep carpet "…I have to protect my reputation." His bitter voice turned her insides. "How much?"

Kate sank into the soft cushions. Weary, she pushed down her pride. He had to know the truth. "I'm in debt, Mack," she said, her voice breaking. "Serious stuff. Up to my neck. In a few days, I won't have a flat. With that gone, I'll have nothing."

Her eyes closed against his cursing. "All right. You want my money? Then it's an exchange."

"Exchange?"

"I support you during your pregnancy. After that, the baby's mine."

Chapter Two

Kate's head snapped up.

She couldn't breathe. Pain suffocated her chest. Sensations of which she was barely conscious burst into her brain. Touching her child's silky smooth skin. Feeling the tight grip of tiny, tiny fingers. Listening to soft, snuffled breaths. The warm clean smell of her baby cuddled against her breast. Her baby. In that instant, the new life growing inside her had never felt so real. And Mack wanted to rip that away. Wanted to *buy* her baby.

No.

"You can't—" The words were strangled and she couldn't stop the tears spilling on to her cheeks. "Mack, no. Please."

His jaw tightened. "What sort of a life would a child have with you?"

Kate's hand shot to her mouth, biting back a sob. "Why?" She wiped her palm over wet, sticky skin. "Why do this?"

"Because I refuse to have you hold this baby over me."

"I would never—"

"Please, Kate, can we not go through the whole innocent act again? We both know you'd use this baby as a pawn."

She could feel the bile souring her stomach. "You really believe that?" She stared up at his stone-carved face. "That all I want, have ever wanted, is your money?"

"You're here, aren't you?" His dark glare drilled her and the stain of hot color rushed under her skin. "See. You've never given me any reason to believe otherwise. So," he straightened and his eyes sharpened on her, "do we have a deal?"

When she'd woken that morning Kate had never intended to give away her child. She had only wanted a little money to tide her over. But reality crashed in. She already worked exhausting hours and she was still broke. She would never be financially equipped to look after a baby, not with Francesca a constant weight around her neck. No home, no money. Mack was right. A baby would have no life with her. She should have realized the impossibility from the beginning. He was her only hope of giving her baby a good start, a proper upbringing. She wished the hollow feeling in her stomach would go, that tears weren't burning her eyes.

But the words wouldn't come. Kate hoped one day her baby would forgive her. And maybe on that day, she could forgive herself. She pressed her hand against her lips and slowly nodded.

Mack turned away. "Christ, Kate, I didn't think I could hate you more than I already did."

Kate stared at his tense back. A test? It had been a test? And she had proven a spectacular failure. She closed her eyes and let out a slow breath. For a brief second, she allowed herself to see a life with her baby. Seeing first steps, hearing those first, precious words. Looking into shining eyes she hoped would be as blue as her own, not—

But then shabby, rented rooms pushed into her imagination, even more crippling debt, as childcare ate into her salary. A future where her baby would hardly see its exhausted mother, become more attached to paid carers than to her.

Whatever was necessary. Kate's fingers curled into her palms and she welcomed the sharp pain. Deserved it. At least their baby could have the undivided attention of its father. "Please, Mack. You're right." She took a calming breath. "Bring up my baby."

"You want me to do this? *Buy* the baby?" He shook his head, raking his fingers through his short, bronze-gold hair. "What kind of woman are you?"

His words were another sharp slap. That couldn't stop her. "I know you never wanted children, Mack, and this is not ideal but—" He stared at her. Or was it that he had never wanted children with her? She crushed the painful thought. "You'll be the sole guardian. I won't contest."

"I should've known better," he grated. "Thinking that there'd be a maternal bone in *your* body."

Kate forced herself onto her feet. All right, she could play on his image of her. She knew now. For her baby, she could do, would do, anything. "You're right." Her voice was steady. Kate amazed herself by holding Mack's gaze, ignoring the disdain she found in their darkness. She was glad she had never told him about how she supported Francesca as her next lie appeared. "I'm only concerned in looking after myself." The lie tightened in her stomach, making her feel sick. "Always have been."

"Yes, I know."

She stared over the hard beauty of his face. Mack had never loved her, she was certain of that now. Kate couldn't believe how her life had spun completely out of control. It couldn't get any worse. "So?"

His next words proved her wrong.

"If we do this, you do realize that we have to get married again."

"What? No." Kate backed away from him, her hands raised. "There is no need for that."

Mack's face was stone. "So I'm supposed to pay my ex-wife for her baby and she conveniently disappears? No, you're not getting off that easy, Kate."

Easy? He thought giving up her baby was easy? She needed to sit down again. Feeling light-headed, she fell into one of the chairs set in front of his wide desk. "This is far from easy."

"And you think I need this?" His face appeared grey and tired. "I woke up in a nightmare two months ago. You, in my bed. And we had…" He sank into a chair opposite to her. "I'd put it from my mind, not thinking there'd be consequences."

"Don't hold back, Mack."

"Do you really believe I want you back in my life?"

"No." She sighed. Tiredness weighed on her, going back to bed felt like a great idea. "This is a mess."

"Yes. It is." Mack straightened in his chair. "But I have to do what's right. A child needs its mother. You're not escaping your responsibility, Kate."

"I never wanted—" Cold eyes made her words falter.

"—to have my baby. Yes. You said."

Those hadn't been her unspoken words. She had wanted to say that she wasn't trying to avoid her duty to her baby. "That's not true." She reddened when Mack's dark eyes narrowed.

"You don't have to butter me up, Kate."

Mack stood, suddenly business-like. She'd forgotten how tall he was, how impossibly handsome. Sunlight edged his sharp features, making his sandy hair gleam gold and bronze. When they had first met, she had laughingly called him a bright and shining Apollo, not realizing then how truly untouchable he was.

He walked slowly toward the expanse of glass, his hands tight behind his back. "I have a reputation to uphold. That's the other reason we have to marry. And I can't simply announce that I've acquired a baby. Not to—" He stopped and she watched him take a sharp breath. "So…" He stared down at the smaller buildings clustered around the tower. Kate felt his mind working, "…we've had a reconciliation. We're to marry again. Quickly. Quietly. No one needs to know about the baby yet."

Kate had to ask the question. "And how does it end, Mack? We can't stay married for the sake of a child."

He didn't turn, but his reflection made her heart squeeze tight. His face shuttered. "My parents managed."

Kate remembered soft words spoken in the darkness, of how his father had married his mother for her money and afterwards broken her with his numerous affairs, how Mack had promised never to be the same. "But what if you find someone? *The* one."

His features could have been carved from granite, there wasn't a flicker. "I never did believe in soul mates." Mack finally stared back at her and she blushed as his eyes traveled down her body to rest on her abdomen. "That small life comes first now."

"But marriage?" Kate dropped her gaze to her knotted hands. "Mack, you hate me." Something inside her shriveled when he didn't deny it. "Our child would sense it. It'd be better for you if I disappeared out of both your lives."

"Selfless Kate Mackenzie."

Fire burned in her chest. He always did this, made her emotions wild. Yet now those emotions were hard, destructive. "Hartley. I changed back." She bit out the words, wanting him to know how little having his name meant to her.

"You surprise me." Absent fingers straightened his waistcoat and he moved to his desk. Mack closed a folder, his hand delaying there briefly. Eyes sharpened on her and he relaxed back into his large, black chair, his face the now-familiar derisive mask. "I thought you were still trading on being the ex Mrs. Sean Mackenzie."

Kate flushed.

She should have known Mack wouldn't let it lie. Nothing would stop him from finding out how his ex-wife had gotten close to him. It was the only time since their divorce that she had used his name.

Francesca had begged her, pleaded with her, for a chance to attend the prestigious Pennington Hoffer Ball. She should have said no. But Francesca was her weak point. Guilt over breaking her promise to her mother always made her agree to whatever her sister said.

Francesca had stormed out after half an hour, declaring that every man was blind as well as stupid. Kate had stayed. And because of one stupid decision she was now sitting in Mack's office. "Once," she said, wanting her voice to be calm. "And it put me here."

"Poor you." There was no sympathy in his tone, or in his face. "Life's always been so hard, hasn't it, Kate? Especially when your meal ticket walks out on you far too early."

"It always comes back to your precious money." Kate stood. She still had her own home for a day or two longer. Crawling into bed, hugging her pillow and crying, that was her plan for the rest of the morning. "Are you happy that I finally have to beg for it?"

"Amazed you stayed away this long, actually." He stared over her loose suit, the mess that was her face and hair. She sharply resisted the urge to touch the tangles, to try to look presentable to his critical eyes. "You always had such *expensive* tastes."

"I never realized the money you gave me was begrudged."

Mack pushed himself away from his desk, his face tight. "Make yourself look presentable. We have to start this charade and I doubt Angela will believe that I'd be involved with anyone who looks the way you do."

Color burned across her face and neck. On leaden legs, she walked back to the window chair to pick up her bag. Her voice had gone. And now they had to tell Angela. She pulled at the bag strap and forced herself to walk to the bathroom. Her world had been turned over, but his attack on her ravaged looks cut deep. She had never been beautiful, not even pretty, not like her sister. Mack had been the only man to make her feel attractive, desirable, and she had loved him for it. In that moment, Kate loathed the father of her baby.

Silently, she closed the bathroom door. Kate stared at the mirror, bright, artificial light shining harshly over her grey skin. "Look presentable." She fished through the small bag for her makeup. "Not going to happen in this lifetime." Powder, blusher, smudges of kohl, lipstick. The result, in her eyes, was only a marginal improvement.

She attacked her straight, black hair with a brush and caught it again in its silver clip. She pulled at the strands of her fringe. "I'm insane to be here, doing this." But she looked down and pressed her hand against her belly, wanting to connect to the new life growing there. She would do anything to ensure that her baby was provided for. All too sharply, she remembered Mack's antagonism and her courage wavered.

No. Her spine straightened. Mack, if nothing else, had always been an honorable man. He would care for her during the pregnancy. She would have her baby, her job at the University. It was enough. It would work. It had to. She had no other choices.

"And here she is."

Nerves clenched at Kate's stomach. Angela was already in the office, frosted brown eyes fixed firmly on her. Mack crossed the room, blocking Angela's sharp glare with his body. "Better," he muttered. "Just. Smile, Kate. If you can't, just think of all the lovely cash that will be flowing through your fingers once again."

"Don't."

His dark brown eyes bored into hers. "Then say you're not here for what my wealth can get you."

Kate wanted to say something, to deny it, but it was true. She was broke. Her gaze dropped away and she felt ashamed.

"As I always thought." He took her hand, and turned back to his PA. "So, Angela, you can be the first to congratulate us. We're getting married."

Kate jumped as Mack brought her fingers to his lips. The soft graze unexpectedly shot heat to her core. Her attention leapt to Angela, catching the rush of disbelief over her smooth features. Dark eyes narrowed on Kate and she flushed red.

"How, Mack?" Angela's gaze slid away with obvious dislike. "Why do this to yourself? Again?"

"Angela."

The gentle warmth in his voice. Kate felt nothing for him, nothing, but still his whisper took her mind back. Murmured endearments, the brush of his lips over her ear, feeling his smile on her skin. She had loved him completely. But that was gone, so much ash...

"It's okay."

"No, Mack. It's not. This woman is a leech—"

"Enough!" The sharp bark made Kate start. Angela blinked. "I want you to organize a quiet ceremony. As soon as possible." His fingers tightened around hers and a tug had Kate moving forward. "Reschedule all of my appointments for tomorrow."

"But, Mack—"

"A.S.A.P., Angela."

They were out of his office and marching through the cube farms to the lift. Kate was aware of the turned heads, the curious glances as their boss strode by, half dragging her. "Where are we going?" she managed to ask as Mack stabbed at the ground floor button.

The lift doors slid open.

"You have to pack and move into my house."

"But I can do that. You don't have to—"

"Kate. You're ill. From now on you will rest, eat properly." Fingers cupped her face, turned her to him. "You're just skin and bone."

She twisted free of his hold, not wanting to see the clinical detachment in his eyes. "It's not that bad. I have trouble keeping some of my food down, that's all."

"It's now my baby." His face was sharp. "And I'm doing what you asked. You want me to support you? Well, I control your life. Completely."

A brief burst of rebellion made Kate laugh. "You're not serious."

Mack's fist hit the emergency stop. Her fingers scrabbled against the support rail as the lift tilted. But it was the fire in his eyes that had

Kate shrinking into the cold, steel corner. Her heart hammered. The lift was too small. Far too small.

"I am not happy. At the minute, I can't think of anything worse than being married. Especially to you." Mack gripped the rail, his body blocking her into her corner. His voice sent unwanted shivers through her as his breath brushed her skin. "There will be no freedom for you, Kate. Not like the first time. I've bought you. I've bought your time." His gaze raked over her face, her neck, dropped further. "Your body."

The heated word made her breath catch in her throat. "No."

"Yes." He stroked her cheek, his fingertip pressing, pulling at her lower lip. His eyes were dark, hot. "You will be whatever I want you to be. Do whatever I ask you to do. The man you knew is gone, Kate."

She stared. "Yes."

"I will protect my baby, but cross me…" He left the threat hanging. "Do you understand?"

"Yes." Kate closed her eyes, not wanting him to see the weakness of tears. "Mack, what happened to you?"

The man pushed himself away and the lift began its slow slide again. His voice was thick with bitterness. "You did, Kate." His jaw clenched before he spoke again. "And I'll never forgive you."

Chapter Three

Kate wrapped her hands around the mug of weak tea.

Mack had sat her on her small, low sofa with the mug and disappeared again into the tiny kitchen. She stared unfocused at the grubby white walls. The threadbare rug scratched at her bare feet. Mack had threatened her. The panic still spurted through her.

They had married in a rush of lust, too fast, without really knowing each other. She had thought him a kind and decent man in the few, short months they'd been married. She had obviously only seen the pleasing veneer.

"Toast," Mack said, presenting the slices on a faded, patterned plate. He sank into the narrow sofa, twisting against the spring she knew poked through on that side. "This place is a dump."

"We can't do this, Mack," she said softly, a piece of thinly buttered toast halfway to her mouth. "Please."

"There is no discussion. This is going to happen. It has to." His face shuttered and Mack was on his feet, too tall against the low, stained ceiling. "Eat that, while I pack. Clothes and personal items. Furniture to the tip."

Kate opened her mouth to argue and found Mack's dark glare. "Why are you doing this?"

A smile twisted his mouth. "Revenge."

Her answer jammed in her throat as he headed toward her bedroom. Her bedroom. Kate struggled up, her cup finding the mantle. Mack was not going to rummage through her things. The phone stopped her.

"Kate. There you are! What are you doing at home?"

"Francesca." The last thing she needed right now was her sister. Kate got to the point. "What do you need?"

"Well, the thanks I get for worrying about you! I phoned that place, whatever it was, and they said you left five weeks ago. What's going on, Kate?"

She sighed and stared at her closed bedroom door. It was too quiet. What was he doing? Mack touching her things. It was wrong in so many ways. Belatedly, she remembered her sister, felt her impatience. "It fell through—"

"Fell through? But I was counting— That's typical. What am I supposed to do now?"

Kate broke into her sister's selfish tirade. She had no nerves left for both Mack and Francesca. "I'm pregnant."

"What?" Laughter crackled through the receiver. "Don't be stupid! You don't have sex, couldn't get it if you tried. How can you possibly be pregnant?"

"Fran." Kate pulled at the curling cord, edging toward the closed door. "I'm sorry. I had to put the baby first. And the morning sickness. Most of the day's gone before I can even think about facing it—"

"But I suppose you'll manage to *drag* yourself in for the first day of term? Hauling your bulk around. But when I need this little favor…" There was a pause and Francesca sighed. "Katie, I'm so sorry. Really. Honestly. It was the shock talking. Of course, your baby has to come first. Auntie Francesca. I like, love the sound of that. It'll be fun. Have you thought of any names yet?"

Kate closed her eyes. Fran's happy, playful voice always made Kate forgive her sister's harsh tongue. She knew she was a pushover, knew it. But Francesca was her sister. They were the only family either of them had left. "Not yet."

"Francesca's a great name," she said, laughter in her voice.

Kate didn't want to smile and bit at her lip to stop it. The smile curved anyway. "But not good for a boy."

"It could set a trend." Francesca paused. Kate's smile faded and she focused on her bedroom door. "What's the father providing?"

Disappointment slipped cold over Kate's heart. Francesca always had to find out how she could benefit. She had actually danced, whooping and waving her arms, when Kate had told her about her marriage to Mack. For the first time. Only sixteen, but her obsession with herself had started young. "We're getting married."

"Married?" Francesca barked. "Why? How long have you been seeing this man? Why didn't you tell me?"

"Francesca—"

"No. I think this is the height of selfishness—"

"It's Mack."

"What? Wait. You can't." Another pause. That surprised her. Kate had thought her sister would have been overjoyed to have access to Mack's wealth again. "You got back together? Kate. Are you sure about this? I mean. Sean Mackenzie. After last time…"

Kate wasn't listening to Francesca's unusual display of concern. She was staring at the man standing in her bedroom doorway, a suitcase in either hand. The anger on his face was all too clear. "I have to go."

"No, wait. Please. When is it? Think about this first. Kate!"

She placed the receiver back onto its cradle, trying to breathe against the tight constrictions of her heart. The cases dropped. Mack took one step towards her and heat flashed through her body. She was trembling, couldn't stop. It was something she didn't want to label.

The ringing phone made her start. Her attention snapped to it, knowing it was Francesca ringing back.

"Leave it."

Kate curled her fingers back into her palm, watching as Mack picked up the receiver, dropped it and took it off the hook.

"You told your sister you were pregnant."

His voice, low, dangerous, leeched under her skin. Her breath was shallow. Mack slowly circled her, prowling, moving too close, his mouth twitching as she shivered when he brushed the soft material of her blouse. His scent wove around her, making her remember too much. Of experiencing the silken strength of his body, knowing how well he knew hers. The feather-light touch of his fingers.

Kate was only able to nod.

"I said no one was to know about the baby."

His fingernail lightly stroked the underside of her jaw and she actually yelped. Her heart pounded. Dark, feral eyes raked over her face, fixed on her mouth. Was this his revenge? Making her want him again? She expelled a ragged breath.

"I don't make idle threats, Kate."

Her pride told her she should fight him. But the emotion she didn't want to label was there, crushing self-respect, dignity, anything stopping Mack from—

He laughed and stepped back. His dark gaze mocked her loss of control. "And I think the punishment was enough. For now. Don't you?"

Shame burned her cheeks and unfulfilled ache beat through her blood. "I hate you."

"You were always so easy, Kate."

Tears. She was tired of crying. She wanted the happy hormones her doctor had promised. The ones letting her glide serenely through her pregnancy. "Then we make the perfect couple." A flush darkened his face and Kate steeled herself for Mack's particular brand of retribution. Kate cursed her quick tongue. "Sorry."

"Yes. I'm sure you will be." A finger slid down the soft curve of her throat and stopped on the rapid pulse in her neck. His hand dropped away and he pulled out his mobile phone. "But I'm saving that pleasure for later. Angela?" He paused, listening, a slight smile tugging at his mouth. The hard mask slipped and with a brief flare of something Kate was not calling jealousy, she watched his dark eyes soften. "I need you to organize a removal firm."

Kate moved away, not wanting to listen to him dissolving her life. She had to get herself under control. But all that she could dwell on was the hot promise in his voice and the way she melted at his slightest touch. Revenge. She sank into her sagging sofa. She picked up the toast and ate it, unthinking. Her first marriage had broken her heart. Kate stared up at the man standing in her front window. Smiling, relaxed, until his attention shifted back to her. Mack stiffened and a hating shutter slid back down over his face. He turned his back on her.

She knew her second marriage would destroy her.

The rapid knock at the front door brought Kate out of her maudlin thoughts. Her gaze snapped to Mack. Was Angela *that* efficient?

"I'll call you back." An eyebrow rose. "Expecting anyone?"

Belatedly, Kate pushed herself to her feet. After what he had said about controlling her life, she realized that she was expecting Mack to get the door. "No." But he was already moving. Kate let out a slow breath. This couldn't get any—

"Is Katie up yet?"

Worse. The bank letter had wiped everything else out of her head. That and worrying about asking Mack for money. She had completely forgotten Robert would be at her flat that morning. And she had asked him to stop calling her Katie. Now it sounded hideously overfamiliar.

"Who are you?"

The ice in Mack's voice shriveled her. She could practically hear the thoughts in his head as he questioned whether he was the father of her baby. She forced herself to walk along the narrow hallway, darkened by Mack's tall frame that effectively blocked the doorway.

"Robert Thorpe." There was the pause she knew was coming. "And you are?"

"Robert." Kate squeezed through, trying not to press her body against Mack's. The edge of the door scraped her hip and she hissed, involuntarily rubbing herself over the smooth heat of his muscled leg. Color crawled up her throat. Now was so not the time.

She was free and standing in front of Mack, glad she couldn't see the cold glare prickling the back of her head. "Robert. Sorry. I completely forgot."

"Katie?" Dark blue eyes questioned her and then shot to Mack. She saw Robert's eyes harden, his normally smiling, mobile face stern.

Her smile wanted to crack away from her skin. "Yes, sorry." She looked briefly up to Mack, but only caught the tight line of his jaw. "Mack, this is Robert Thorpe. Yes, of course, he just said. Doctor Robert Thorpe. We work together, well not actually together. In the same department, I should say." She took a calming breath and willed her heart to slow. "Robert, this is Sean Mackenzie."

Mack's hand fixed to her shoulder, a heavy, implacable weight. Fingers curled into muscle and bone and she had the sickened thought of feeling branded. "Kate's fiancé."

Robert's dark eyebrow rose. "Fiancé?" A smile twitched at the corner of his mouth. "You'll do anything to avoid me, won't you, Katie?"

Horror tightened around her heart. Not his sense of humor. Not now. Pain sharpened in her left shoulder. Mack's fingers digging. Robert's gaze shifted there and narrowed. The shock of pain eased and Kate let out a heated breath. She slipped a waxen smile over her mouth. Hide in her tiny bathroom and cry. That was her silent wish. "You know me, Robert," she murmured. "Work comes first."

"Not anymore." Mack brushed his fingers along the gentle slope of her shoulder. Kate shivered against the warm caress.

Robert straightened and his dark blue eyes sharpened with suspicion. Kate held down a sigh. The man had become almost overprotective since her "illness" had started. She hadn't told Robert she was pregnant. Telling him would necessitate explaining *how* she had gotten pregnant and by whom. And she wasn't ready to explain that, even to herself.

"Well, I should congratulate you both." There was no warmth in Robert's smooth voice. A smile curved his mouth. It almost looked real. Almost. She jumped when he took her lax hand, squeezing gently. "I'll call you. Later."

"She's moving out."

Mack's words spiked in her gut and Robert's hand tightened in reflex to the harshness in the man's voice. "I'll be in touch," Kate said quietly.

"Katie?"

Damn it, the man was digging a deeper hole for her by the second. "I'm fine, Robert." She made a smile work over her lips, had to make him believe it or he would never leave. She extracted her hand from his and let her fingers lightly stroke Mack's hand as it rested on her shoulder. "And glad to be getting out of this dump."

The smile Robert settled on her was warm, made contagious by the flash of dimples. "About time." His attention slid back to her hand on Mack's and moved over her head. There was a wary coldness in his dark eyes. Almost a warning. "Take care of her."

"I don't need to be told that."

Kate heard the repressed anger in Mack's voice. She was sure none of this stress was good for her or the baby. She waved a hand back into the flat. "We still have a lot to sort out, so—"

"Yes." Robert stepped reluctantly away from the front door. Tightness gripped his tall, muscled body. Yet another problem she did not need. "I will see you, Katie." He nodded briefly. "Mackenzie."

The door to her flat closed and it had the hollow bang of a jail cell. Her mouth was already working. "It's not what it looks like."

Even in the dimness of the hallway, fire sparked in his dark eyes. She backed up against the door, felt the metal edges of the letterbox cold into her spine.

"And what does it look like?" The rage in his soft voice spiked her heart. "Tell me that, Kate."

"Robert's a friend. He was already a lecturer at the University when I started my PhD."

Mack blinked. "PhD?"

Kate grabbed at the chance to change the subject. "Yes. I got a first and my tutor said I had the aptitude to go further. So I—"

"No."

Mack moved close and Kate hissed against the cold bite of the metal into her skin. His heat washed over her, she could almost feel the touch of his body over hers. So close. His warm, intoxicating scent wrapped around her senses. She had the sudden, insane aching need to rub herself against him. Satisfy— Her mouth dried and all she could feel was the frantic thud of her heart.

"You're not squirming out of this. Is he the father?"

"Of course not! I have never slept—"

"Sleeping was never your particular skill, Kate."

She closed her eyes. She didn't want to fight, picking at the freshly exposed wounds. "Is the deal off?" His silence had her heart sinking. Well, she could beg a mattress on the floor of Robert's neat little flat. At least she knew that now.

"You won't see him again."

"Mack, there's never been anything with Robert. I work with the man. How…" Her words faltered. She stared up at him. He wasn't backing out. "I promised that I'd work the semester, or at least do as much as I could. My due date is the first of March."

Something flickered in Mack's eyes and was gone. "Work? No, that can be another promise that you don't need to keep."

A hollow fear filled her stomach. He couldn't take that away from her too. "I—"

"This is something else not up for discussion. You'll be my wife."

"What kind of Neanderthal are you?"

His large hand briefly framed her jaw and the anger bled from her. She had to remember to breathe. But it was difficult when his other hand slipped tight over her hip. A gasp escaped as he dragged her hard against his body.

"Do you want me to show you, Kate?"

"Mack."

His thumb traced over her lip. "I told you, you're bought goods."

"No. Not like this."

"Yes."

Kate wanted to fight him, she did. But her rebellious body remembered Sean Mackenzie, demanded that he rekindle the fury of passion that had blazed between them from the very beginning. The flames already licked low in her belly, flickering, burning. She groaned as he thrust his leg between hers, knowing how, oh God, knowing where…

She devoured his mouth. All anger, fear, self-respect, forgotten. The sweet, dark taste of him, his tongue, lips, biting fingers on hot flesh scorched desire through her. She had to have him, feel him…

With a curse, Mack tore himself away and wiped the back of his hand over his mouth. "You really are something."

Kate watched the desire die in his eyes and it turned her own need to ashes.

A hard smile twitched at his lips. "Trying to convince me that I got my money's worth?"

Her soul was lost, still lost in her physical need for Sean Mackenzie. She closed her eyes. Now Kate *knew* it couldn't get any worse.

She was wrong.

Chapter Four

He hated her.

Mack's fierce strides ate the length of the hotel corridor and beat out that thought in his brain. For seven years, Kate had been a burning rush of anger searing his gut. And yet here he was, about to marry her. Again. He tugged at the tight collar of his shirt. The damn thing felt more like a noose. A grim smile twisted his mouth and he saw one of the scurrying maids flinch.

"The things I do for my family," he muttered.

It had been nine days since Kate dropped her particular bomb. Nine days since he'd seen her. Mack had installed her at his house, told his housekeeper to take particular care of her, and moved into his city apartment. Kate wanted his money? Fine. It didn't mean he had to—

He scratched at his hair, wincing as nails scraped against his scalp. Mack knew why he had to stay away. Kate Hartley was under his skin, in his veins, from the very instant he'd met her. Still there. Even that brief taste in the shabby hallway of her flat—

No. She would not fool him again. He'd care for his baby.

Mack's long stride faltered.

Kate was having his baby. He crushed the sprig of warmth that grew in him at the thought. The damn woman had *sold* him his own child.

Keep those thoughts nice and angry. He rapped on her hotel room door. "Kate, it's me." He twisted the handle and froze.

He had forgotten. With her hair scraped back and that God-awful blue suit she'd been wearing, he had forgotten. He stared. Fresh, summer sunlight flooded the room, bathing Kate in gold. Her shining black hair, loose and falling around her bare, pale shoulders. The delicate profile, beautifully enhanced by a skilled hand. And the dress. In his anger, he had deliberately chosen something simple, almost plain. But on her… Mack's gaze dropped to her abdomen, wanting to see evidence of his baby. Only a slight swelling, but to know—

Reality hit him. The man holding her hand was not one of those hired for Kate's hair and makeup.

"Why didn't you tell me, Katie?" His soft, sympathetic words made Mack's hands tighten into fists. And did he have to keep using that annoying diminutive? "I can help. You don't have to do this. My family's finally starting to sort itself out. I've been promised—"

"How touching," Mack said.

The look of guilt on Kate's face made his smile sharpen.

"Mack—"

"Trying to play me for a fool? Again?"

"It's not—"

"What it looks like? Yes. You've said that before. Strange how it keeps on *looking* so damn suspicious."

"Robert was leaving." Her hands were already on the man's back, trying to push him toward the door. Mack would have laughed normally, Kate's little stick of a frame trying to heave out such bulk, but there'd never been anything remotely funny about his dealings with Kate Hartley. "Weren't you, Robert?"

"You don't have to marry him, Katie."

"*Kate* asked you to leave." He met the man's dark blue eyes, finding distrust and a sharp dislike. "And now I'm *telling* you to leave."

"You can't force her—"

Mack couldn't help the laugh that erupted. "I assure you, Dr. Thorpe, I'm a most reluctant bridegroom." Thorpe's eyebrows drew together and Mack felt his sudden uncertainty. "Kate and I will have a very civilized arrangement. But it will *not* involve you. Am I making myself understood?"

Kate answered for him. "Perfectly," she said. She turned to Thorpe and the hard edge softened. "I don't need a white knight, Robert." A smile pulled at her mouth, something regretful, resigned. "But thank you." She sighed. "Go. This is something I have to do." Mack knew she wanted to say more, knew it when her blue-violet gaze shot to him and her lips parted.

"You know where I am. Day or night."

Thorpe's heroic posturing was beginning to grate. Mack held open the door and gave the man a hard smile. "We're running late. And we don't need another witness." His smile grew. "Or do you want to give me the pleasure of throwing you out?"

The man's face was stern and Mack had a sudden rush of recognition. But then Thorpe was speaking, his voice low, angered, "You don't deserve her."

Mack found Kate round-eyed, high points of color breaking through the dusting of powder. The rapid pulse beat at the base of her throat. Guilty fear? Had she snared another man? Fury burned at the thought. "I know. But then no one does." He stared at Thorpe again, his voice sharp. "Now get out."

Kate's small hand slipped into his, slender fingers tightening into his palm. Mack resisted the urge to stare at the false symbol. "Robert, this is getting silly."

Thorpe ran a hand through his dark hair and a wry smile cut his mouth. Damn it, he looked like someone, someone Mack should know. "I worry about you, Katie."

Her fingers clenched. "Francesca put you up to this, didn't she?"

A brief flicker of something like guilt crossed Thorpe's face, and another flash that Mack couldn't name. "Call me."

Finally, he was gone.

Mack closed the door. He had to remind himself why he was doing this. For the child. His jaw clenched. And for his grandfather.

Kate yanked her hand out of Mack's tight grip.

"I didn't tell him to come here. How could I? I didn't even know where I was going until your chauffeur pulled up outside this place."

She sank with relief into a white rattan chair and closed her eyes, willing her breathing to slow, to find calmness. She hadn't been nervous until Robert's sudden and unwanted appearance in her room ten minutes before. She'd had a quiet, even pleasant week rambling around Mack's large house, eating the housekeeper's excellent meals and actually feeling well. Then Robert, doing the knight in shining armor routine. For Mack to find him there.

Kate opened her eyes. He was staring at her, waiting, his long body taut. He had not bawled her out, or declared the wedding off. "Why do you still want to marry me?"

A smile twisted his mouth and he raked long fingers through his bronze-gold hair. "Despite your attempts to throw another man in my face?"

She was calm, she was. He would not make her mad. Kate let out a slow breath. She would get business out of the way. "I've signed all your papers." She waved a hand at a pile of legal documents sitting on the dressing table. "Your solicitors were very thorough, but they want you to look over them too. Make sure everything is in order. I know what I'm expected to do—mother, nanny, possible arm ornament." She watched his eyes narrow. "Shouldn't I be allowed to know why you're *so* willing to carry on with this charade?"

"I'm marrying you, Kate." Mack wrapped his fingers around her upper arm. "Your child will have my name and you'll have access, albeit very limited, to my money. There's nothing beyond that."

Kate stood and Mack released his tight grip. "So—"

"Discussion ended." He picked up the papers. "Let's get this farce over with."

Anger had made his voice clipped, his movements sharp. Kate preceded him, silently, out of the room. She tried not to remember the first time they married and failed. The ceremony had been in a hotel too. But there, the similarity ended. There was no holding hands now, or the inability to stop grinning, looking at each other with eyes bright with love. Kate swallowed and blinked away embarrassing tears. She was remembering a teenager's fantasy, a whirlwind rush of her youth and his hormones.

"Kate. It's here."

She stopped and turned to the door. It hurt, like a knot of pain in her stomach. She didn't realize her hand was shaking until Mack took it, linked his fingers through hers. He felt warm, strong. The knot twisted. She would not cry, she wouldn't. But her eyes burned, and her throat ached. Why couldn't she be indifferent to him and see this as a convenient business deal? But, despite how he acted, how he treated her, it was Mack. Kate closed her eyes. Her body, her heart, still ached for him.

"Ready?"

For the baby, she told herself. She could do this for their baby. "No." The word was out before she could think. Kate risked a glance. Mack's dark eyes were unreadable. "Are you sure you want to go through with this?"

His bark of laughter cut. "Trying to make me think you're human, after all?" His fingers gripped her palm. "No, I don't want to do this. I *have* to."

Kate looked away, ashamed that she had to do this to him. "Mack—"

"Do you want to know why?"

She couldn't speak.

He took her silence as an assent. "My grandfather wants me settled." His voice was bitter. "He sees too much of my father in me."

A man like Mack, marrying because he was told to? And marrying her? "But that wouldn't—"

"Kate. Accept that I'll marry you. Again. My life beyond that is none of your concern." With that, Mack opened the door and waited for her to precede him.

Kate stared around the small, sunlit space, saw the solicitors who were to witness the wedding. The registrar had the only genuine smile in the room.

"You've found her," she declared.

"My reluctant bride," Mack said, with a grin Kate would have sworn was real.

She stumbled forward and found Mack's hand at the small of her back, bleeding warmth through to her skin. She sucked in a breath. If she could survive this, then the worst part of the day would be over. Mack had made it obvious that he didn't want to spend any time in her company. It would be a relief to be alone.

The ring.

Everything else shot out of her head. A plain, white gold band. It looked... It was. But he wouldn't. *Her* ring, the one Mack had taken back.

"Surprised?"

For some reason, he had to have a wife. Would he have used her ring then? Kate remembered to breathe. "I shouldn't be."

The rest of the ceremony was a blur. All that Kate could remember were a few mumbled words on her part, and the ring. Feeling its alien weight, the smoothness of the icy gold against her skin.

She watched Mack's long, brown fingers curl away from the wedding band, the one that bound her to him as his wife. She should be staring into his eyes, falling into his dark gaze. Finding love there. But Kate couldn't look up. Sean Mackenzie didn't love her. He was marrying her because he had to. A wry smile tugged at her mouth. And her wedding ring knew.

"...I now pronounce you husband and wife."

The touch of Mack's fingers on her jaw made her stomach clench and she fought back the sting of yet more tears. Now for the perfunctory kiss. The one to satisfy the onlookers, to perpetuate the charade.

Time slowed. His sharp, intoxicating scent wove through her as he drew closer and slid his hand slowly along the plane of her jaw, slipping behind her ear, fingertips easing into her hair. Kate tried not to feel the pained thud of her heart, the anguish tightening her stomach.

She would not cry. She would *not* cry.

The warm brush of his lips over hers. The shaved smoothness of his skin. A gentle pull on her lower lip, and the sweet, dark taste of him. It was not enough. Kate allowed herself to find the starched coolness of his shirt collar, to stroke nervous fingertips over the warmth of his neck.

She couldn't stop it. A tear escaped and coursed, wet and cold, over her cheek.

Kate knew Mack had tasted it. Saw it in the way he pulled back. And then his touch was gone from her skin, his fingers retracting from their intimate but impersonal hold. A second tear followed the path of the first. She stared up at his face and her heart lodged in her throat. Sean Mackenzie was beautiful, his features carved as finely as any Greek sculpture. Bronze-gold hair, always in a rough tangle, fell onto his browned temple, making Kate's fingers itch to stroke it back into place. His eyes. Those eyes had haunted her dreams for years.

A muscle jumped in his sculpted cheek. Did her tears embarrass him? Destroy the image on which they had both agreed? Namely of a couple in love, happy at the prospect of finding each other again, after years apart.

Kate turned to walk back past their witnesses, her arm automatically sliding through his, her fingers tightening into the sleeve of his expensively tailored, black suit. She barely heard their congratulations, the swift conversation as Mack passed back the signed paperwork.

She started at his warm breath over the shell of her ear, leaning close. Kate found she was holding her breath. Stupidly, she wanted him to whisper the endearments he once had.

"What are you playing at, Kate?" His voice was bitter. "Tears? You're not living up to the ideal of the happy little bride."

At that exact moment, Kate didn't care. The simple ceremony had her drained and defeated. Stupid to want him. Stupid to— No, she couldn't even think that *other* word. "See them as tears of joy." She wanted to curl into the back of the car that would take her to Mack's house and sleep away the afternoon. Alone.

"Your bag's been packed," Mack said. "But there's still a change of clothes." He unlocked the door and she gratefully collapsed into one of the big, thickly cushioned chairs beneath the windows. She kicked off her tight shoes and rubbed at aching toes.

"Thank you," Kate murmured. "Now we can go back to our separate lives."

"No."

Her head snapped up. "I signed the papers. It stated discreet, separate living arrangements."

"It will be. After the honeymoon."

"Excuse me?"

"Get changed, Kate. We have a plane to catch."

"No, no, no!" Panic gave her energy. She was on her feet. "There was nothing in that phone directory about a honeymoon. I would've remembered that part."

"Calm yourself, for the baby's sake." Mack eased her back into the chair. His words made her flush with guilt. "It's expected. The weekend. Nothing more."

"Where?"

Why wouldn't Mack look at her? "My grandfather's estate, in Northumberland."

Things began to slot into place. "You want to parade me." Kate tried to be calm, but anxiety and fury knotted her insides. "What the hell are you getting for being married, Mack?"

"I told you, that's not your concern." He straightened and held her gaze with a hard, uncompromising glare. "Now get changed."

                 ℰℴ

Kate stared up at the beautifully proportioned, neo-classical mansion. Sunlight gleamed over white stonework, reflecting the summer-blue sky in the box sash windows. Had Mack had grown up there? She realized he had hardly ever talked about his childhood. There'd always been that closed look shuttering his face and she had never wanted to pry further.

Mack strode across the crunching gravel. Kate followed him.

They hadn't done families the first time around. Not properly. Mack had only briefly met Francesca. Kate winced at the memory of her sister asking her new brother-in-law how much he was worth *exactly*. Francesca had then seized on the opportunity to go to an exorbitantly expensive private school.

Kate had met none of his relatives. Until now.

She sucked in her courage. He had promised her they would leave on Sunday evening. Just the rest of Saturday afternoon and one more full day. She could do that. She hoped. Kate rubbed her thumb at the underside of her rings. He had given her back her old engagement ring on the short shuttle flight.

She was making an unnecessary fuss. It was simply Mack's grandfather. Some old dear who had a strange notion about how to see his grandson happy.

The double doors opened before they reached the first step. "Mr. Sean." A grey-haired man in a neatly pressed suit gave Mack a deferential nod. "Your grandfather is expecting you in the Summer Room."

"Both of us, Reeves?"

Kate blinked. No polite conversation, not even a smile for someone who appeared to have been a long-serving family retainer.

The man's pale gaze snapped back to Mack. "Mrs. Mackenzie—"

"Dr. Hartley," Mack broke in.

Kate wasn't imagining the trace of satisfaction in his voice. She had wondered why he had agreed to her name staying the same. Yes. There was a whole layer to her marriage she knew nothing about.

"—is invited to attend," the man finished, as if Mack hadn't spoken. He stood back and Mack ushered her through, into the marble-floored entrance hall.

Kate tried not to stare at the portraits, the sumptuous furniture, tried not to let the grand scale of the rooms overwhelm her. She had known nothing but her shabby little flat for too many years. It was still disconcerting to be thrown back into how the wealthy lived.

The Summer Room was a large, wooden conservatory, warm and slightly humid, filled to bursting with orchids. Kate was too busy admiring the beauty and color of the delicate flowers to notice the man approaching them.

"So this is it."

The sharp voice made her jump. Kate turned to find a tall, white-haired, elderly man. He walked with a cane, but his back was ramrod straight. She met cold blue eyes and held down a shiver. Definitely *not* an old dear.

"Kate, may I introduce my grandfather, Colonel Greville Mackenzie? Colonel, this is my wife, Dr. Catherine Hartley."

"Wife?" His pale gaze slid to her hand, narrowing on the rings they found there. "A wife has your name, boy."

Anger spiked in Kate. She realized where Mack got his winning personality. "I'm doing perfectly well with my own name, thank you," she said, her voice barely controlled. Mack's hand closing around hers caught Kate by surprise. A gentle squeeze urged her to be calm.

The Colonel ignored her. His attention fixed again on Mack. "Let's hope you can keep hold of this one," he said. He turned away, his cane tapping against the tiled floor. "No wife, no deal, Sean. Try to remember that." He rested his cane against one of the long tables and picked up a pair of secateurs. He looked back and a white eyebrow lifted. "Why are you both still here? Dismissed."

Kate seethed. She knew her cheeks were flaming. She glared up at Mack and found him white-lipped, fury snapping in every movement of his body. She almost had to run to keep up with his fast, angered pace. Reeves was waiting for them at the bottom of the wide, curving staircase.

"Your luggage has been put in the Blue Room."

Mack nodded a brief acknowledgement before he took the stairs three at a time, leaving Kate far behind.

She grabbed at the smooth banister rail, her head light. She calmed herself past the sudden dizzy spell. "Damn it, Mack," Kate grated, breathing hard as she reached the landing and found Mack halfway along it. "I don't know where I'm going."

But he didn't wait for her, slamming his way into a room somewhere on the left. "Lasting until Sunday..." Gingerly, Kate peered behind one door, finding a broom cupboard. "I can't see us staying here till tea time."

She opened another door. Blue shimmering wallpaper, velvet, blue curtains. "The Blue Room?" Kate closed the door on the elegant little sitting room and spied her unpacked bag, standing beside a dressing table in another room. No sign of Mack. But there were other doors. Kate rubbed at her tired face.

There was a large four poster in the corner, draped with rich blue silk. Plump pillows, a heavy throw. Kate kicked off her shoes and shrugged out of her jacket. Mack could do what he liked. She was sleeping.

ॐ

"Kate?"

She batted at the fingers touching her cheek and rolled away. "Sleeping, Mack."

"Kate, wake up."

Mack? Her eyes shot open. Mack. Married. Odious grandfather. She covered her eyes and groaned.

"You have to get ready for dinner."

"I am not going anywhere near that horrible old man," she said, pushing herself up and leaning heavily into the piles of pillows. She dragged her hair from her face.

"This is not open to negotiation."

His grandfather's words came back to her. "What deal, Mack? What am I securing for you?"

He let out a slow breath, staring down at the heavy throw mangled on the bed. "I had to get away before, because I wanted to pound *something*. The old," he spat out a curse, "has tried to rule my life from the very beginning." A twisted smile pulled at his mouth. "I can't remember a time when I haven't hated him."

"You just ignored the question."

Mack looked up. His mouth twitched. "Yes."

She was smiling. Why was she smiling? Her heart skipped when he unexpectedly mirrored it. For the first time since they had been reacquainted, she saw the man with whom she had fallen in love. And there was not one trace of the waspish Colonel in his features. "Mack."

The smile fell from his mouth. He turned away and began to pace. "It's Saturday. The Colonel usually has a bunch of his local cronies dine with him. His 'Regimental Dinner', he calls it. Just smile and stay calm."

Kate stared at her hand, the soft light playing over the facets cut into the solitaire diamond. She held back a sigh. "I'd play this game better if I had any idea about the rules," she said quietly.

"Make small talk. Stay polite. My grandfather's not particularly fond of women. He'll ignore you." Mack's face was hard. "Role number three, Kate. The arm ornament."

Kate forced herself away from the comfort of the bed. Her feet sank into the deep carpet and she stood straight. She should have known their marriage would be so…clinical. "What kind of role models are we going to be to our child? Running the cycle. You treating me the way your grandfather treats you."

"Look at me."

Something cold passed over her heart at the frozen tone to his voice. It had been an idle comment. Reluctantly, Kate did as he said.

The fury she found in the man made her fingers curl into her palms. She had never seen him so angry.

"I am *nothing* like him," he grated, blood burning in his face.

Kate stared. Had he always been so volatile, so willing to burst into flame? Her heart pounded at his rage. She tried a smile. "I ramble for a living." She was talking to his back, because he strode toward the wide window. A tense silhouette against the blue sky.

"He threatened to evict my mother."

"Excuse me?"

Mack didn't turn. "Unless I married and proceeded to," his voice took on the clipped, bitter tones of his grandfather, "'bang out some decent heirs', he would evict my mother." He let out a slow breath. "She lives in a lodge on the edge of this estate."

"But you could easily afford—"

"My grandmother let her live in the house after my father died. A car crash. Him and his latest mistress." Mack's jaw tightened briefly before he continued. "The house was a shell, but my mother rebuilt, refurbished it. She's been there for twenty-five years. It's her home. I've offered. She doesn't want to budge and I couldn't force her. She doesn't know what that old man has threatened to do." Mack rubbed a hand over his face. "My father bled her dry and broke her. Her cottage gave her back some of her self-confidence." His voice lightened. "She learnt to lay bricks, she's a mean plumber, and what she can't do with plaster."

Kate slipped her hand into his, looking up at him as he continued to stare out over the gardens. "You just had to tell me, Mack," she said, her fingers tightening through his.

He turned his face to hers. "I can't trust you."

The words were a punch in the gut. She had wanted to offer comfort, had seen him in pain. Damn him. She pulled her hand free. Damn him and his whole bloody family. "So," she swallowed and prayed her voice wouldn't break, "you told him I'm pregnant?"

"I wouldn't give him the satisfaction."

Mack didn't know he could hurt her. She was someone he hated, just like his grandfather. A figure of hate had no feelings to wound, obviously deserved everything they got. Yes, he was too much like his grandfather. Kate stared down at her abdomen. She hoped that particular aspect of Mackenzie DNA had passed her baby by.

"Dinner," Mack said. The word was thrown away as he headed for the door. "Formal wear."

"I don't—"

"I took the liberty of getting you a dress."

"Yes, I forgot, you control my life now."

"Correct," he said. "And you're not to tell anyone about this."

"Who am I going to tell, Mack? I'm practically in isolation."

He stopped, turned to her. Dark eyes held her, making the blood bake in her face. "Not quite." His gaze moved slowly over her sleep-rumpled blouse, the creased skirt. Unwanted, her skin burned. This was more of his need for revenge, playing with her need for him.

"Now, get dressed." His eyebrow rose. "Or is this delay an invitation?"

She clearly wasn't obeying his demands quickly enough. "Invitation?"

The curve of a sharp smile cut his mouth as he opened the door. "Obviously, we have yet to consummate our union."

And then he was gone.

Kate rushed at the door and slammed it. She tried not to see the tangled sheets twisting over the wide mattress, to imagine those sheets wrapped around their very naked bodies. Angry with herself, she cut out more traitorous thoughts. What was she doing? Mack hated her. Kate sank on to the bed and pressed her hands over her face, fingers tight against her eyelids. She would *not* cry. She wouldn't waste any more tears on that man.

But they still leaked.

The day couldn't get any worse.

Chapter Five

Kate skimmed her fingers over her sharp collarbone. She was still too thin. She let out a slow sigh. Could she do this? Sit and be polite, be calm for an odious old man and his cronies? Her fingertips slid over the smoothness of her skin and shook with a slight tremor. Her nerves were shredded. She stared at the image in the mirror, the sprawl of their bed behind her. Worry gnawed again. The main fear being where Mack was sleeping.

"No. Not going there." She refocused on her image in the long mirror. She was too pale, her dark hair twisted away from her neck, exposing more white skin. Makeup concealed some of her weariness. But the dress. Red silk, fitted a little too snugly over her breasts, creating curves on her thin body. She splayed her hand over her belly, wanting to believe there was a growing, soft roundness.

"I will keep my head down," she murmured. "Be the simpering decoration, as stated in the contract."

A wry smile cut her mouth. Decoration? "I'm not even pretty."

A sigh swelled her chest and she turned away from the mirror.

"About time," Mack muttered, opening the door to the bedroom. "We're late."

Kate stopped. And stared at him. She hadn't been thinking. Of course, it would be a formal occasion. Her heart crushed tight in her chest and her mind filled with a memory before she could stamp on it. Hard.

The Pennington Hoffer Ball. Weaving unsteadily towards the bar, a smile hovering over her mouth. She had always loved black-tie affairs, because Mack looked positively edible.

Her smile fell away. Too much alcohol flowed through her veins. She knew that as the aching sense of loss tore through her. For a moment, a brief, stupid moment she had forgotten. Again. He wasn't hers. Never had been hers. Tears pricked her eyes.

She ordered another drink and almost lost herself in it, before she caught a flash of bronze-gold hair. The sharp, too-familiar profile. Her mouth dried. Mack. Damn it, he was leaving. Before she realized, she had slipped off the barstool and was moving through the laughing crowd, oblivious to them. If she could only speak to him, maybe the pain would lessen. Maybe.

She caught his arm, felt the cool smoothness of expensive cloth. Her heart hammered. He turned. She saw the blaze of fire in his dark eyes.

"Kate?"

Her mind snapped back. "Yes, yes, I'm ready." She preceded him into the long corridor. What was she doing? She was simply a convenient pawn in Mack's game with his grandfather. She was stupid to think there could be more, stupid of her to *want* more. "Why me?"

"I would have thought it was obvious." Mack stared at her abdomen.

Damn, she had muttered those words aloud and he had misinterpreted them. Her mind stumbled for a reply. "But…but surely there are scores of women who would—"

"You were always my first choice, Kate," Mack said. "Even before."

She stared up at him, her heart thumping. "What?"

"I would never inflict this on another woman."

Kate fought the pain swelling through her. A monster sat behind Mack's handsome face and she should loathe him. She should. Yet, it wasn't that easy. She dropped her gaze.

"The guests are arriving." Mack's voice was calm, obviously not caring about the impact of his terrible words. His fingers slipped beneath her chin, lifting it, and Kate forced herself to look at him. "Smile. Be polite. My grandfather's bad enough without you causing a scene."

On slow feet, she made her way down the wide, marble staircase, her small heels clicking. An evening with Colonel Greville Mackenzie could *not* be any worse than spending five minutes with his grandson. Kate belatedly stitched a social smile onto her mouth. A couple had been ushered in by Reeves, a ruddy-faced man in his early fifties and a much younger, darkly beautiful woman.

"Sean, we weren't expecting you," blustered the man. "Does the Colonel know?"

"Yes, he does, Major." Mack smiled down at Kate and a lump lodged in her throat. His eyes shone, his happiness actually looked real. Vainly, she wished she were as good an actor. "Kate, may I introduce Major Sir John Charlton and his wife, Lady Anthea." His arm slid around her waist and Kate resisted the need to melt into his warm, secure touch. It was false. All false. "Major, Anthea, this is my wife, Dr. Catherine Hartley."

Kate accepted the surprised congratulations, politely kissing them both. The Major declared that they needed to celebrate and led the way into the softly lit drawing room. He left them to "round up a suitable bottle" from the caterer, but was waylaid by another guest. A tall, golden-haired older woman, with a soft, natural beauty that had Kate's stomach crawling with envy.

"Wife, Mack?"

Kate's mind jumped back. She caught the slight widening of Anthea's beautiful eyes, the curve of her smile. But a hard glint cut her dark gaze. "And you vowed to stay a bachelor." Was that something in her voice, too? An edge of disappointment?

She stopped herself from flinching when Mack's arms slipped, slid around her waist and his long fingers idly caressed her hips, her abdomen. Warmth bled through the thin silk and involuntarily she bit at her lip. His subtle, spiced scent tightened the muscles low in her belly. Kate desperately concentrated on not letting her eyelids drift down, to sink back against his hard body. She knew what he thought of her, how he felt. However, in that moment, it was the furthest thing from her thoughts. She was insane, insane to melt at his slightest touch.

"The right woman made me break that vow."

Kate covered his hand with hers, following his slow, sure stroke.

"So that wasn't your first wife?"

Mack's hand froze, tightened. The words burned through Kate, and her sudden desire fell to ashes. His touch dropped away. But his voice was calm, even pleasant. "Kate *is* my first wife." He waited a heartbeat. "The Major seems to have forgotten all about us and our drinks."

He gave them both a brief, tight smile and followed the path the Major had taken.

"You're very brave," Anthea said.

Kate stared at her. "Excuse me?"

The bitter burn of embarrassment had fallen from Anthea's features and was replaced with an attempt at concern. "To try marriage for a second time." She glanced at the delicate, platinum watch on her tanned wrist. Her fingertips ran over its intricate bracelet. Anthea looked up and false pity shone in her face. "The Major..." She glanced at her animated husband. Kate saw no warmth, no love there, "...tells me Mack had to marry."

Kate's gut twisted. Did everyone know she was a paid bride? Calm, she was calm. "How so?"

Anthea blinked and her eyes widened. The look of disbelief was calculated. "Why, to cover his indiscretions." More sham emotions flitted over her perfect face. "I'm sorry," she said, and rested a long, taloned hand briefly on Kate's own, "that you had to hear it from a stranger, but Mack takes after his father. Women are *too* interesting." She leaned in close and Kate held her breath against the strength of Anthea's perfume. Her voice was little more than a whisper. "He even tried to seduce me."

Kate bit back the question burning on her tongue. Had he succeeded? Instead, she smiled. "I entered this marriage with my eyes open, Anthea."

"Then we're both practical women, Kate."

"So it would seem."

"And we find our...pleasure...wherever we want." Anthea's eyes bored into hers, glittering with determination. "With *whomever* we want."

A single thought revolved in Kate's head. Mack...had...with this harridan. Oh, God. Was he still with her? The pain was swift, sharp and stabbed at her insides. But not her heart. Not there. Those feelings for Mack didn't exist. Not anymore.

"Here you are, red for Anthea, and a mineral water for you."

Kate's head snapped up. Saw the smile, the shine in his dark eyes. Was this how his mother had always felt? She was his wife, but he wasn't her husband? The ache of that realization, knowing that she still wanted what she once had with him.

"Kate, are you all right?"

She gave him a waxen smile. "Yes, fine, thank you." She took a hasty gulp of the cold water to stop herself from gabbling. She was stupid. Stupid. Completely. Utterly.

"Kate was just telling me how much she's looking forward to reveling in your wealth."

Horror shot through Kate. Anthea's voice was playfully pleasant and her smile wide and sharp. Kate had *never* wanted to punch anyone more than she did in that moment. Calm. No scenes. She was not making it worse. She made a bright smile cut her mouth and linked her arm through Mack's. Her stomach knotted as his forearm tensed beneath her fingers. But her smile didn't falter. "The money is only the icing, Anthea." Kate pressed closer into Mack's hard, unmoving body. "That must be obvious."

"I want to introduce you to my mother," Mack said. "Excuse us, Anthea."

Kate cringed at the cold tone to his voice. She caught the triumph in Anthea's face as they turned away. "Hideous woman."

"The Major's besotted with her," Mack replied. "Can't see that she married him for his title," eyes flicked to her, "his money."

"I didn't say anything."

"Keep conversation to the weather, teaching. Innocuous subjects. You will not discuss us."

Kate resisted the urge to scrub at her face. "Now I have to play nice with your dalliances?"

"What?"

"That woman said—"

"Later." Mack cut her cold. He stopped. "Mother."

Kate blinked. The tall, blonde women to whom the Major had been talking smiled at her son and enveloped him in a tight hug. She should have seen the likeness. It was Beth Mackenzie.

"It's been too long," she murmured.

"I phone."

A wry smile lit her face and the resemblance to her son was startling. "Not the same as seeing you, Mack." The smile faded and her gaze slid down to Kate's abdomen. Delayed there, then lifted to hold her in a cool stare. "So, we meet at last, Kate."

He'd told his mother about the baby. Heat flared in her face. Yet another woman who believed she'd trapped Mack. She had thought she might have some affinity with this woman, but it was obvious to Kate that her son was her darling. She held back a sigh and put out her hand. "Pleased to meet you, Mrs. Mackenzie."

Beth's hand closed around hers in a cool, light grip. "Yes," she said.

"The Colonel doesn't normally invite you to this event, does he?" Mack thrust his hand into his pocket and stared around the room. Kate had the distinct impression that he didn't want any conversation to pass between his mother and herself.

"A last minute invite."

"Since we turned up?"

"Greville wants to rub my face in you getting married again. I always said you wouldn't." That twist of a smile, the one her son had inherited, lit her face. Her gaze rested on the sour-faced Colonel. Beth's smile grew. Kate found him glaring at them, at her. "I think he's just heard who Kate is."

Greville Mackenzie marched across the drawing room. His knuckles stretched white around the cane, which he seemed to use more as a rod for his anger than as a support. Cold blue eyes fixed on Mack. "This woman is your first wife?" Aware of his guests, his voice was pitched low, but the veins stood out on his withered neck. He was almost shaking with rage. "What are you playing at, boy?"

Mack smiled, but it didn't reach his eyes. "Kate and I resolved our differences."

The naked fury on Greville Mackenzie's face made Kate wince. She was already feeling heartily disliked by everyone she met. Why did *he* object to her so strongly? The Colonel turned his fury onto her and all trace of humor fled. Unconsciously, she shrank back into the protection of Mack's body. Was Mack's reaction equally unconscious? Holding her close, so she felt safe, completely safe.

"She won't carry on the Mackenzie name." The Colonel's gaze narrowed and spat ice at her. "She won't even take it as her own."

"Enough!" Mack grated. "Kate is my wife and deserves your respect."

His anger sounded real and something inside of Kate fractured. More lies. The Mackenzies seemed to revel in playing games. She was tired of it. Well, this was her life. Her *baby's* life. She straightened and took Mack's hand. "If you will both excuse us." She met the Colonel's fury and her heart pounded, but she did not look away. "It's a pleasure to talk with you, as always, Colonel Mackenzie." Deliberately, she looked from him to Beth, and Kate was surprised to find a brief shine of approval in her eyes. Kate's smile became genuine. "And to meet you, Mrs. Mackenzie."

"Call me Beth."

Kate turned away, her hand firm in Mack's. "Is he apoplectic?"

"Foaming." There was satisfaction in his voice.

She stopped at the cloth-covered table and accepted a fresh glass of mineral water from a smiling waiter. Her hand trembled. "You have to tell him," she said. Kate took a sip and the water ran cold down her throat. She pressed the glass against her flushed cheek. "He'll find out soon enough."

"Let my mother goad him a little first." His finger brushed a droplet of water from her skin and Kate shivered at the gentle caress. "I'd forgotten how fiery you can be."

Words failed her. That particular gleam in his eye had always set her heart racing. Liquid heat curled, twisting low in her belly. How did Mack do this to her? He was using her, the Major's wife was hinting and there was his PA, Angela. It hurt, stabbed, but when Mack was with her, touching her, that knowledge fled. She'd been denying it. As she'd tried to deny her pregnancy, but this was as real. She loved him. She had never stopped loving him.

Gratefully, she heard the call for dinner. "We should be going."

"Kate?" The softness of his voice tightened her heart.

"I'm hungry, Mack." Her heart splintered when his hand dropped away.

&

He saw her seated and Kate spread the linen napkin over her lap with trembling fingers. She focused on the gleam of the crystal glasses in the golden candlelight. Mack sat on the opposite side of the long wide table, several places to her right. He was too far away and she felt bereft. Major Charlton bustled into a seat on her left, smiling at her.

"Not your normal wedding reception," he said, pouring her a glass of water.

"No." The rest of the guests were pulling back their chairs, the warm air filled with polite chatter. High French windows had been thrown back to the just-darkening, late summer sky. A light breeze drifted through the long room, bringing with it the soft scent of mown grass, a host of sweet-smelling fragrances from flowers she couldn't identify. "But it's nice."

"Tonight is a special night." The Colonel's clipped tones cut the warm, glowing air.

"Or it was," Kate muttered.

"My grandson, Sean, was married this morning." There was a surprised ripple of conversation, followed by a brief burst of clapping. Greville Mackenzie's smile was sharp. "To Dr. Kate Hartley," he ground out her name. He paused. "Doctor of what, exactly?"

Her cheeks burned. He was determined to embarrass her in front of his friends. "English," she said, her voice clear, strong.

"So not a *real* doctor, then."

"Grandfather," Mack grated.

"Just wanted to be sure," the Colonel said in an over-pleasant voice. "Kate is Sean's first wife, though with all the women in the world to choose from, it escapes me why choose someone as stick-thin, ugly—"

"Colonel!" Major Charlton protested.

Kate's hands tightened around the napkin. She remembered to breathe. Horrible, horrible, old man. Her chin lifted and she found the Colonel's cold eyes, ignoring the smirk cutting his mouth. Kate pushed herself onto her feet and anger burned in her gut. She was speaking before she realized. "Not stick-thin for long." Her hand splayed over her abdomen. "If you get my meaning."

Shock sat on the old man. His mouth opened and shut, but there was no sound.

"Kate."

She jumped at the hand on her arm. Mack. Her heart sank. She had just blurted out that she was pregnant.

"Let's go."

They walked out of the silent dining room. Beth brushed her hand over her arm and Kate caught her sympathetic glance. No doubt Beth would stay for the fallout.

Mack closed the double doors with a heavy thud.

Catering staff still buzzed about the drawing room. He stopped one of the waiters and asked him to send their meals to their room. The stern set of Mack's features froze the questions on the young man's mouth.

Kate's heart hammered. Was he waiting for the privacy of their room before he bawled at her? She dug fingers into the soft flesh of her palms. She had handed that hideous old man the one thing he wanted. And she knew Mack would be furious. But those seconds of shock, when she'd stunned him, had taken the sting out of his hateful words and had brought her a satisfied glow.

Mack slammed the door to their small sitting room. Kate's heart rate jumped. She watched him tug at the tight knot of his bowtie and fall into a blue damask armchair. His hand scrubbed at his face.

"It just came out," she said, wanting to speak, to explain before he started to harangue her. "I needed to shut him up."

"Damn it, Kate. I specifically told you—"

"And I was supposed to sit there and take *that*?"

"Stupid words, from a stupid old man."

Kate sank into the sofa and kicked off her shoes. He used to know how sensitive she was about her looks. Now he had forgotten. Or didn't care. Slowly, she pulled the clips from her hair and sighed at the warm weight around her shoulders. She stared at the clips, twisting them in her fingers, watching them catch the light. "Do we have to stay here?"

"Kate—"

"Seeing him gloating at breakfast. Slapping you on the back."

"I have to act the dutiful grandson, you know that."

"If your mother knew what your grandfather was holding over you…"

The sudden fury in his face stopped the rest of her sentence. "Don't even think of telling her."

"I just thought—"

"Do I have to buy your silence? Is that what this is about?" Mack stood and began to pace. "I should have known better than to trust you with that information. But then I keep forgetting what kind of woman you are."

Anger made her hands clench. Muscles tight, she rose from the sofa. "And what am I?" she demanded.

Mack raked his dark gaze over her and her skin flushed. "The color fits." She held down a shiver at the icy burn of his eyes. "A siren, a demon. Tormenting me."

She couldn't help the bark of laughter that escaped her. "Hardly."

Her amusement made something harden in Mack's face, intensified the fire in his eyes. "Playing innocent?" The softness of his voice sent prickles over her skin. He moved closer and Kate had to stop herself from backing away. Her heart hammered. "And all the while, scheming, finding weaknesses."

His thumb traced the thin strap of her dress, followed it down over her breast. His touch on her bare skin, smooth, skimming, made her head light. Kate had to remember to breathe. "I should have realized what a formidable opponent you were, from the very beginning."

"Mack."

"But you had a veneer of fragility. So beguiling."

Circling her, his fingertips stroked her skin. His mouth close to her ear, the heat of his breath, the almost press of his lips. Kate's legs ran liquid. Damn it, he could *not* do this to her. She couldn't let him create this need, this ache to have him. Right there. He traced the shell of her ear with his tongue. Kate gasped.

"But so wanton." His fingers tugged at the zip low on her back.

Rational thought burst back into her brain with the cool wash of air over exposed skin. "Mack, this is wrong." She pulled free, desperate to hold the loosened dress. Something still burned in him and it made her take a nervous back step. "You know that."

"Since when has that stopped me?" His smile was wicked and his dark gaze slid over her legs, over her hips and stomach, narrowing on the hands that clung to her dress. Finally, it reached her face. Her skin had scorched in his wake and now she met his fiery gaze. Kate tried to deny what it did to her, the rush of heat under her skin, the sudden need pulsing through her veins. She tried to deny it. And failed.

The red silk of her dress slipped from her fingers.

Chapter Six

Kate's skin prickled again at the path Mack's gaze took, as they lingered on the swell of her breasts. His sly, appreciative smile made her mouth dry. She couldn't have been more aware of him if that firm mouth had slid, hot and wet, over her burning skin. Oh God...

He towered over her. His eyes held her. Kate stared, transfixed. Something about Mack moved past her sense of reason. Instinct was taking over again.

His darkened gaze returned to her mouth. He wet his lips and a spike of excited anticipation stabbed at Kate's gut. Mack moved closer. Touched her. But not his mouth. His hand stroked her jaw. Yet, even the simple caress of his callused fingertips had her blood fizzing. Kate closed her eyes against his touch. His touch. She'd been barely able to contain herself when only his eyes had scorched a path over her body. Now, the need for more of him was her only thought, pushing against his palm, her lips, tongue, tasting him.

"You have no power over me, Kate." His voice was almost hoarse. "I'll show you how little."

"Yes." She was only half listening. "Kiss me, Mack." She sounded brazen, but she had never wanted anyone but him. The need scared her. Her eyes opened at his delay. "Please?"

Mack's thumb brushed her lip, his eyes narrowed, almost black. "Don't forget, I know what you are," he whispered. There was derision, but also something else she couldn't name.

"Mack." Her fingers swept down his hand, his arm. She discovered warm skin under his shirt, losing herself in touching him. Smooth skin over taut muscle. A light dusting of hair over his stomach, her fingers ran further, over his chest, teased a tight nipple.

With a low moan, his mouth covered hers, devouring her. Lips, tongues battling. Hot. Furious. Anger burned away under passion.

This couldn't be happening. Kate tried to tell herself that. Even as Mack grabbed her, desperate to press her against his erection. Even as her nails raked his back, clinging to him, cursing the barrier of his clothes. His mouth pulled away, lips against her cheek, her jaw, until his tongue flicked at her earlobe. She shuddered and gasped into his throat.

"You liked that?"

"You know I do."

He ran urgent fingers over her body, stroking his fingertips up her spine. Kate's skin burned and she moaned into his neck. Her lips slid over Mack's throat, his bristles searing were they touched. It had been inevitable, beginning with her name on his lips. A pleasured ache rose at the thought it would end that way too.

They stumbled and Kate's bare back found the wall, cool plaster a shock to heated, damp skin. Mack crushed her to him, his hips hard against hers. Kate spiraled out of control and then there wasn't enough of him to touch, to kiss, to lick. Somehow, his mouth found hers again and she drowned under the taste of him.

Breathless, he pulled back. "Bed," he muttered, his eyes black with desire. "Now."

Kate's heart was thumping. She told herself it would be only sex. She didn't love him. She didn't. She had to be wrong. Only she would be stupid enough to fall in love with a man like Mack. Again.

There was a blur of lips and frantic fingers. Kate broke away at the bedroom door, jerked it open. The door clicked shut and her thoughts vanished. Mack's arms wound around her waist, pulled her against him

"This can't be denied, Kate," he murmured into her ear. "But it's only sex."

For a brief second her heart contracted. "Yes."

His breath caused havoc on her skin, sending ripples of pleasure through her body. Too long without this, far too long. Vainly, she wished that she could grow used to it. But she knew what this was. Mack had spelled it out. A burst of lust. He brushed the bare skin of her shoulders, making her quiver. His large hands slipped down her arms, his fingertips deliberately stroking, teasing her sensitive flesh. She focused on the rumpled bed.

Mack turned her and his gaze slid down her nakedness. "What should I do with you now, Kate?"

Kate closed her eyes, enjoying the awareness of his voice over her flesh. "What would you like to do?"

"Don't tempt me." His hands slipped over the smoothness of her skin. Further words lost themselves in an openmouthed kiss sliding over her neck and collarbone.

Kate gasped at the sweet torture. Her world shifted out from under her as Mack swung her up into his strong arms. The bed was close. She slid from the heat of his body to sink into the rich softness of the thick blankets. Feather light touches over her throat, chest, so gently over her breast and hardening nipple that she moaned against him. Over the slight swell of her stomach, circling her navel. Fingers delayed over her abdomen. He looked up.

Mack made her heart stop. The gleam in his eyes caught her breath. No one had ever looked like that. Not for plain, skinny Kate.

"Time for you to lose some clothes too, Mack."

She let out a slow sigh. It had to be just physical, for her sanity. She watched him undo button after button, revealing a smoothly muscled brown stomach. His trousers followed. Lamplight streaked his skin with gold. Mack was lithe, beautiful, perfect. She curved her lips into a smile. It faded when he didn't return it.

"Is that enough for now?"

He crawled achingly along her body and she shivered against the slight brush of his warm hand against the coolness of her leg, of his thigh over hers. Her gaze held his. "For now," she whispered. She could lose herself in the darkness of those eyes. *Don't think it's more than just sex,* she reminded herself sharply. There had always been a fierce attraction. This was simply lust.

Lust.

His lips were soft, exploring her throat, drifting further down. Kate ran her fingers lazily through his short hair, sighing at the silken touch. His tongue flickered against a taut nipple. Kate arched into his mouth, fingers tightening, wanting more of this man. How could she not love someone who made her feel like this? No. No more thoughts like that.

Mack's eyes blazed over her soul.

"Mack, what is it?"

No reply. Just the hotness of his mouth slipping, sliding over her stomach, touching her navel, going lower. And then the first stroke of his tongue. Her mind spiralled, her body shuddering, writhing against him. "Oh God."

Kate was still trembling when Mack softly kissed his way back up her body. "Did you enjoy that?" She released a slow, satisfied sigh. "I'll take that as a yes."

"Yes," Kate repeated, her brain still buzzing. She could love him. Quite, quite easily. "'That way madness lies…'"

"Kate, you're having conversations in your head."

Her skin flushed a deeper red. She lifted an eyebrow. "Your turn."

Now she could truly appreciate his body. Replace old memories and the half-haze of that hotel room. Kate straddled him, pressing against his erection. Mack moaned, his mouth urgently seeking hers.

"Not yet," she murmured into his mouth. "I want to return the favor."

Her lips brushed over his hot, salty skin, teeth tugging briefly at a nipple before she continued her descent over a muscled stomach that shivered under each kiss. She breathed in his scent, drawing it deep into her lungs. She closed her eyes and a sad smile tugged at her mouth. He even smelled beautiful. She slipped her fingers into the band of his shorts, eased them down and threw them at the pile of clothes on the floor. Her tongue flickered over him. Mack groaned and twisted up to meet her mouth. Her confidence grew.

"Kate. Stop." Mack's fingers lifted her chin. His eyes were darker than she had ever seen them, his hair disheveled. "Not like this. I want to be inside you."

The desire in his voice made her stomach grow weak. She smiled and crawled back up his body. Crushed against him, Kate reached for his mouth, wanting to lose herself in another one of his dark kisses. She ran her fingers through his hair, driving his mouth harder against hers. Her heart was beating fast, loud, and she was sure Mack could feel it.

His hot skin rubbed against her, a delicious shiver running through her as his hair-roughened chest brushed over sensitive nipples. His moans drowned in her mouth as Kate teased him with her body, enjoying the power she had over him, the ability to make him tremble at her slightest caress. His earlier words burst back. She *did* have power over him.

Suddenly, he rolled her and pinned her arms above her head. His lips broke from hers. Disappointment swept through her, twisting her stomach. Had he changed his mind? Reluctantly, she opened eyes.

"That's better," he murmured.

Kate met his dark gaze. What she found there made her throat dry. Such raw desire. She had never believed anyone could want her that much.

"I want to see me in your eyes."

Kate tried to wonder what he meant but thought disintegrated at the press of him, hard and hot against her flesh. She needed him inside of her.

There. Almost there.

Her body arched, desperate for more of him, holding him deeper. A satisfied moan escaped her. She barely heard his sigh. God, he felt good. She smiled as she looked into his beautiful eyes, holding his gaze when he began to rock slowly against her. This was what making love was supposed to be like. Kate sighed and reached for his cheek, his jaw, gasping when his lips ran over her palm. Nothing existed beyond him. What he was doing to her body. His eyes. God, his eyes seared her. Too much.

Kate shut her eyes, unable to let his soul-stealing gaze read her. Read her heart. He wanted sex. Nothing more. Kate let herself ride the rising tide of pleasure that swept in waves up over her pelvis, stomach, breasts, with each thrust. Forgetting everything, everything that hurt her.

Kate's head felt light, fused. She was so close now, so very close. Kate dug in her fingers, shifting her legs, wrapping around his back, allowing him deeper, harder. The brush of him over her taut nipples made her cry out. Mack's tongue teased at her earlobe.

She was gone. Her body bucked. Kate pushed hard against him, intensifying the orgasm that rioted through her. "Mack..." she moaned, clinging to the man as the tremors rippled over her body, wanting to take him with her.

His fierce mouth found hers through the final few erratic thrusts. "Kate," he sighed against her lips.

They rolled over in a tangle of damp, hot limbs and Kate brushed the sweat-darkened hair from his brow. Her smile wanted to break away from her face. She held his dark eyes, needing to lose herself in them as easily as she had lost control of her body. But he was already pulling away, his face cold, shadowed.

"It was just sex," he muttered.

Kate's heart was a stone in her chest. Numb fingers dragged a sheet over her nakedness. Just sex. Just an angered release. He pulled on his clothes, his back to her. God, he was a true Mackenzie. Heartless. Brutal. She wiped at the tears, desperate for Mack not to witness that weakness. Damn him. He had all the power, the power to make her want, need, love him, after all he had said and done.

"Mr. Mackenzie?"

A young man's voice.

Kate's fingers tightened in the covering sheet. She remembered where she was. His grandfather's house and they had walked out on dinner. "Food." She watched Mack leave the room without a backward glance. "Now I have to sit and eat with him." Kate rubbed at her eyes one final time and reached for her clothes.

∾

Mack watched Kate stab half-heartedly at a roast potato. Damn it, he had had enough of this last night as she'd pushed peas around her plate, made an excuse and escaped to her bedroom. Breakfast had been no better. "You have to eat, Kate." He couldn't keep the anger from his voice. "You're wasting away."

Spots of color rose in her pale cheeks but she didn't look up. "I still haven't got much of an appetite."

"You have the baby to think about."

"I know what I have," she muttered.

"Look, what happened—"

"Have you finished that, Kate?" Beth reappeared from the kitchen, laden with a home-baked, spiced chocolate cake. "You should eat more."

A small smile cut Kate's mouth as she looked at his mother. "I know. At the minute I'm lucky to find anything that doesn't disagree with me."

Beth laughed and started to cut the cake into heavy slices. "It's no consolation, but I was ill for the whole nine months with that monster."

For a brief second, Kate's gaze met his, the first time since they had slept together. But the connection was gone. Damn it, it had only been sex. Something they'd never been able to deny. And now Kate was acting as if he'd *sullied* her. Fire burned in his gut and he glared at Kate's bent head. He bristled with the urge to haul her out of her chair, press her to the nearest stretch of wall and remind her exactly how she'd been a very willing participant.

"Cake."

His mother cut into his heated thoughts. Mack watched Kate excuse herself and disappear from the sunny dining room.

"Stop glaring at the girl. No wonder she can't eat."

"Changed your tune, Mother?" He picked up a dessert fork. "Last week she was a 'money-grubbing harridan'."

Beth hushed him, her gaze darting to the open door. A red stain cut across her cheeks. "That was before I met her. She's not what I expected."

"And what was that?"

"Something worse than Anthea Charlton." Beth waved her fork at her son. "But Kate stood up to the Colonel. That always impresses me." She stared back at the table and groaned. "I've forgotten the coffee again."

"Another sucked in by her 'honest' charm."

He ignored his mother's parting glare. "Play nice. I taught you better manners."

Play nice. He thought his mother would have seen through Kate Hartley. Well, he was no longer fooled. Not anymore. He watched Kate slip back into her seat. Afternoon sunlight shone over her loose, dark hair, catching the edge of her sculpted cheek and making her pale skin gleam. He followed the sliver of golden light as it molded the soft pull of her blouse around her breast. He had lost himself in her body. The experience with Kate, he had never known anything like it before her. Or after.

But sex didn't mean feelings. He had loved her once, fallen for her at the first smile. But that was the past. The woman herself had obliterated any love he had once felt and it was gone now, so much dust.

And what was she doing with that cake? "Are you expecting it to bite?"

Kate stopped poking at the thick icing. A smile curved her mouth, but her eyes didn't leave the plate. "Dangerous things, chocolate cakes. They can strike without warning."

"Then it's wise not to provoke them."

Her gaze found his. Something sparked there. "It's a lesson I should learn." She speared a piece of cake and smiled as she slid it past her lips. The tip of her tongue tasted her top lip, licked at a smear of chocolate. "But not today."

"Are you finished?"

"Still got a whole slice to get through."

Mack resisted the urge to rake his fingers through his hair, fought the ache to have her again. An act. An act to make Beth think that she was a poor little girl trapped by her unfeeling son. Damn the woman. Was he the only one who could see through her?

No. There was one other.

&

"First baby photo."

Kate stared obediently at the black and white photograph. A small, chubby, pale-haired baby lying on a mid-grey blanket, dark eyes fixed on the camera. The suggestion of Mack's adult features were already evident. She itched to trace over the photograph, finding them with her fingers, but she stopped herself. Kate wondered how much her baby would look like the little cherub in the old photo, and how much of the Mackenzie personality it would inherit.

She smiled belatedly as Beth turned the page, trying to show enthusiasm. His mother was showing her a kindness Kate had not expected. But her mind was on the man in the chair opposite, the one who had glowered at her all through lunch. She had thought to lighten the atmosphere with a touch of teasing, but that had backfired. Kate could feel the enmity pulsing off him. She didn't want to label it hate. Stupidly, she loved him. Her gaze involuntarily turned to his as Beth chattered.

Fire burned there, his mouth stern. Her insides twisted. He never smiled at her. With an angry flick, he turned over the page of the Sunday broadsheet. His eyebrow rose, mocking, and she shot her attention back to the photographs. Her mouth started working. She had to put Mack out of her mind.

"He looks familiar."

Beth paused. "That's Edward, Mack's father."

"No. Him." Kate lightly touched the image of a man standing next to Edward Mackenzie. Tall, dressed immaculately in an expensive suit, dark haired. He was smiling and Kate could just make out piercing blue eyes and dimples. Dimples just like... "Robert Thorpe." Kate closed her eyes. Why had she blurted out that name? The rustling of the newspaper stopped. Kate silently cursed her own stupidity.

"Robert Thorpe?"

Kate heard it then. The sudden worry in Beth's voice. She saw the woman's fingers whiten on the heavy page. "I work with a Dr. Robert

Thorpe." She shrugged and knew that Mack's gaze drilled her. She couldn't look at him. "It's just a vague similarity—"

"The family named a nephew after Robert, the year he passed away." Beth's voice was soft, hinted at an old pain. "The Thorpes are an ancient family. Connected to the hilt, rich as Croesus." A smile tugged at her mouth. "Have been fighting about that money for too many years."

"Doesn't sound like the Robert I know," Kate said, wanting to end that particular conversation. Beth was hurting. And it was the truth. Robert lived simply in a small flat, drove a beat-up old car. There had never been any mention of a wealthy side to his family. In fact, he usually avoided any talk of family. It was an uncomfortable subject for him. "Are there any more incriminating pictures of Mack?"

Beth was quiet, her fingers delaying on Robert Thorpe's face. "What?" The page turned too quickly. Her smile was forced, too bright. "Yes. There's always the obligatory bath picture."

"Wonderful," was the mutter from behind the newspaper. "Leave me some dignity, Mother."

"You know that the reason a parent takes these pictures is purely to embarrass." Beth gave him an indulgent smile. "You were very cute though."

Mack glared at her over his newspaper, but there was a shine of humor. "You're biased."

Beth's smile grew and Kate saw the shadow lift. "So sue me."

She had a sudden stab of envy for the close bond Mack shared with his mother. Her own mother had always favored Francesca. The "little doll", as her mother had called her. Even as she lay dying, wasted by cancer, her final thoughts had been with her second daughter.

Kate had clung to a thin, yellowed hand, trying not to cry, trying to be strong. That was what was expected. She was seventeen, an adult. She was the sensible one. Capable, dependable.

"You're the strong one, Kate," her mother said, her voice rasping. "Francesca's a silly little girl. An innocent. You must look after her in every possible way. As I would."

As I would. The words that drove Kate to penury.

"Kate?"

She blinked. Beth's sunny front room slid back into focus. "Sorry." Her gaze shot to the empty chair. "Where's Mack?"

"Bringing the car around. I lost you there for a few minutes."

"Sorry."

Beth put the photograph album on the low coffee table and climbed to her feet. "I know there have been problems in the past and I'm glad you've sorted them." She gave Kate a warm smile. "But you mustn't let Mack bully you."

She didn't want this conversation and was incapable of replying to Beth's kind words. Her emotions were already too close to the surface. Bursting into tears was the last thing she wanted to do. She fought back the stupid, stupid impulse to throw her arms around the woman and sob out the horrible truth of her marriage to Mack.

Pregnancy hormones. They were messing with her head. Kate willed herself not to be emotional. Instead, she smiled. "I can stand up for myself."

"Good," Beth said. "Mack has gotten his own way for far too long." She stared down at Kate's abdomen. "And I haven't asked. How many weeks are you?"

"Eleven."

Beth linked her arm through Kate's, guiding her along the sun-filled hall to the front door. "Dry toast first thing in the morning stopped the worst of the sickness. For me. Didn't help in the afternoon, or the evening though." Kate forced herself to match the woman's bright smile. "When's the first scan?"

"In three weeks." The first scan. Something else she had put from her mind. That and telling Mack about it. Would he want to attend? Watch the life they had created wriggle on a black and white monitor?

"Safely delivered."

Kate found herself being passed on to Mack. "Thank you for a lovely lunch, Beth."

"Get my son to visit more often."

"I'll try."

"Now I have to get started on my leaking roof."

"I said I'd pay," Mack said.

Beth glared at her son. "I'm perfectly capable of fixing a few slipped tiles."

"Remember to take some provisions." His grin was sharp. "In case you get stuck."

Mack opened the passenger door to the Jaguar and Kate slipped onto a cool, leather seat. The slam of the driver's door reminded her to put on her seatbelt.

Mack gunned the engine and skidded the car over the short gravel path, earning a farewell shout from his mother. Kate relaxed back and closed her eyes. Now, if Mack would maintain his brooding silence she could sleep away the time to the small, private airfield, forget—

"Another award-winning performance."

Kate ignored him.

"You had my mother eating out of your hand. I should've given you more time with the Colonel. He'd be no match for you."

The acid in his voice burned through her. "Have you finished?" Kate twisted away from him, as far as the seat belt would allow. She stared, sightless, at the countryside as it flashed past.

"Just complimenting you on good work."

"Should I do the same?" She held his angry gaze. "After all, *that* wasn't in the contract."

"The sex was always good," Mack said, his eyes back on the road. His hands flexed around the steering wheel. "It was the rest of the marriage that was shot to hell."

"And whose fault was that?"

"You tell me, Kate. Which one of us married for money?" His cold voice sharpened her anger, showing her again how hopeless loving him was. "Has done it for a second time?"

Kate turned away. She would stay calm. Try to. But the words slipped out. "At least I was faithful."

"What?"

"Faithful," she repeated. Her voice broke on the word and she swallowed. "Like father, like son."

"What the hell are you talking about?"

"I know about Angela, about Anthea."

"Anthea? Anthea *Charlton?*"

He was glaring at her, a flush darkening his face. Kate glanced anxiously at the road ahead. That car was coming up fast. "Mack, now isn't the time—"

"You started this."

Her heart was in her throat. Her hands tightened around the edge of the seat, knuckles white. "Watch the road!"

Mack's gaze snapped forward. Cursing, he brought the car under control with a sharp twist of the wheel. Tires screeched. The blaring horn of the oncoming car ripped past them. He eased on the brake. The vehicle slowed and with it her racing heart. Her terrified grip on the seat eased.

Mack pulled onto the side of the road and wiped a hand over his face. "Damn it, Kate." His gaze raked over her. "Are you all right?"

"Fine," she said, straightening in her seat. "Let's go."

But he wasn't letting the subject drop. "Why on earth would you think that Anthea and I—"

"Because she told me!" Kate let out a calming breath, forced out the next words. "This is none of my business. Forget I ever brought it up."

"She *told* you?"

Kate closed her eyes. "I really—"

"What did she say?"

More icy anger. It made her heart pound. Anthea's heavy scent invaded her memory and the long talons clicked again on Kate's bare arm. The words came out. "That you seduced her." Kate winced against his cursing.

"Why would you believe that?"

"Why would I not?" Kate caught her fingers in her hair. "We're going to miss the plane."

Mack dismissed that with an angry slash of his hand. "I own it. It won't leave without me." He turned her chin to him. Fury tightened his face. "Is that the sort of man you think I am? A philanderer? Like my father? Unlike him, I planned to honor my marriage vows."

Where was he getting all of this righteous anger? Damn him, he thought she didn't know. "I saw you."

"With Anthea?" He barked a laugh.

"No." Her heart was tight. Despite the years, the memory was still too fresh. The scattered papers, strewn across the floor, his desk. Seeing his fingers caught in long chestnut hair. A mouth, which the night before had lingered on hers, with the promise that he would love her, only her, now devoured another. Kate cut out the image. Her voice was calm. He would never know how much he had hurt her. She would never give him that power. "With Angela."

Something flashed through his eyes and his fingers curled away. "Angela."

Without another word, the car pulled onto the road. Kate knew that Mack couldn't deny it, justify it. But didn't she deserve some explanation? She risked a glance at his granite profile, the tight set of his jaw. Obviously not.

Chapter Seven

Kate slid out of the taxi. It was still quite a hike to Mack's apartment, but she needed fresh air to wipe the fog from her brain. She walked slowly along the sunny pavement, enjoying the slight breeze lifting her loose hair. For a few seconds, she forgot why she was making this trek. But only a few.

Angela Craven's terse voice was still with her. Kate had telephoned Mack's office, wanting to tell him about the scan, to ask if he wanted to go with her. Beth's words had stuck in her head. It was another thing she couldn't delay.

"He's taken the morning off," Angela said. "He didn't detail his movements. I assume they're personal." The line went dead.

Seeing Mack in his apartment couldn't be worse than talking to Angela. Not after the heated words in the car the day before. Kate told herself she was being the strong one, keeping to the contract. But the truth was, she needed to see Mack. He had dropped her off at the house and sped away. Not a word had been uttered on the plane, or in the car waiting for them at the airfield. She had to try to resurrect something from the ashes of their relationship. For their baby.

"Who am I kidding?" she muttered. "I want what isn't there. For him to love me."

Kate ran fingers through her hair, realizing that she had to stop talking to herself in the street.

The apartment building loomed before her. Classically over the top Victorian architecture, with one of the most exclusive addresses in the city. A smile tugged at her mouth. Kate had always liked the building, loved the fact that she had lived there.

Her attention returned to the busy road and she waited for the lights to change. She saw someone emerge into the sunlight. Caught a flash of bronze-gold hair. Kate remembered to breathe. It kept surprising her how beautiful he was. Especially now. Dressed casually in black jeans, boots and a dark shirt. Kate blinked And a leather reefer jacket.

That jacket. She knew that jacket. Her mind threw her back to the first time she'd seen it.

A shadowed storeroom, golden slats of hot sunlight striping the floor, the musty scent of paper. Her first day and her first task, sorting the stationery room.

"Who are you again?"

Her mouth refused to work. She stood, her fingers tight around boxes of rubber bands, staring like an idiot at the most beautiful man she'd ever seen. The bands of light made his bronze-gold hair gleam, edged the hard planes of his face. But his eyes were liquid black, almost lost to shadow. Then she remembered that he'd asked her a question.

"Summer temp." She swallowed, wanting to lose the breathy quality to her voice. "I was told to tidy." She realized she was crushing the cardboard boxes between nervous fingers and piled the boxes neatly on the nearest shelf. "To tidy the stationery."

He moved towards her. Kate tried not to back into the metal shelving, needed to glue her feet to the floor and try to be pleasant, professional. The soft scent of leather. The hint of an expensive cologne. And something else, something that made her heart thud. *She swallowed again and fixed a smile onto her dry mouth. "D'you want me to help you find something?"*

A smile pulled at his firm lips and heat shot to her cheeks. No man should be allowed to look that good. "My PA needs staples."

"You run errands for your PA?" The words had escaped before her brain could kick in. "I mean—"

"Shocking, isn't it?"

His velvet voice eased through her. The smile widened and he was close. Too close. His scent wove through her brain and Kate tried to deny the ache low, low in her belly. Boys had never affected her before. He caught her gaze, held it. Not a boy. Kate licked at her lips. Her heart pounded. So not a boy.

The slow stroke of his thumb against her skin was almost hypnotic. Kate melted at the simple touch. She closed her eyes.

His fingertip lightly traced her bottom lip and she shivered "Soft." His voice was dangerously close. "Do you taste…"

Was she imagining the brush of lips over hers? Reluctantly, Kate opened her eyes.

His eyes gleamed as he watched her. Blood rushed under her cheeks when he pushed back her hair from her face, his fingertips caressing her skin. They trailed her neck, burning wherever they touched. "Sweet."

There was a promise in his voice that made her mouth dry. She found her own voice. "Not that sweet." Kate's breath caught at the smile those words drew from him.

He placed a soft kiss on her mouth. And then another. Kate allowed her fingers to touch his jaw, run along the sharp angle. An innocent kiss, but why was her head light, her limbs weak? Madness. It was madness. But she didn't cry out, push him away. Couldn't.

His hands moved slowly over her back, drawing her close. She ran her fingers through his smooth hair, stroked the warm skin of his neck. It wasn't real. She was asleep at her desk. Hot, burning kisses pulsed along her jaw, her neck, back to her lips. "Open your mouth."

It was a dream. So she obeyed. Slow, sensual, his tongue flicked against hers. A gentle game. She pressed against him, feeling the lean hardness of his body. His fingertips drifted over the shell of her ear and a fire-heated ache burst through her body. Kate clutched at the soft leather of his jacket. She had to have more.

She slid her arms down his back, slipped beneath his shirt. The skin was warm and silken beneath her questing fingertips. She had never felt such a rise of desire at the simple touch of a man. And she wanted more than gentle kisses. Kate held him, moved against him in a slow rhythm, instinct trying to satisfy her need.

His mouth was suddenly no longer playful, but drove hard against hers, wiped all other thoughts from her mind. Large hands molded her to the hardness of his body. She met his passion. There was nothing but his fierce mouth and the fire burning under her skin, through her veins, wherever he touched her. Desire washed through her brain as his leg thrust itself between hers, making her fully aware of the hard length of his penis.

Sense screamed at her to pull back, but the aching need to—

He tore himself away.

Frustration. What the hell? Hot shame flooded her and her trembling fingers tried to tuck her blouse back into the band of her skirt. "I…" What could she say? Sorry, I just threw myself at you?

"What's your name?" Gentle fingers lifted her chin, his thumb softly stroking.

Yes. They'd exchanged saliva but not names. Kate cringed.

"No. Don't think this is wrong." His voice, easing warmth through her overwrought nerves, washed her with a strange relief. "This was inevitable." His wry smile lifted her heart. His beautiful eyes examined the dark, quiet room. "What I didn't expect was the cliché of the stationery cupboard."

"I..."

"Lost the ability to speak? Damn, I must be good."

Kate laughed. And fell stupidly in love. Had never fallen out of it...

Her arm began to move, about to wave, but Mack was enveloped in a hug from a tall, dark-haired woman. His arms wrapped around her. Automatically. It wasn't Angela Craven. Not her. Oh God. Kate's arm fell to her side and she ignored the furious beeping of the lights, indicating that she could cross. She watched the woman's lips brush all too slowly over his. Pull at his lip.

Kate's mind kicked in and her heart snapped, splintered. Something died inside her. It was Francesca. Her sister. Her *sister*. And Mack. Kate watched them as they walked away, oblivious. Francesca's arm through his, her other hand playing with the soft leather of his sleeve. Everything so familiar... Laughing, chatting, Francesca being at her most relaxed and charming.

Kate stumbled away, walked blindly. Found herself on a bus. Getting off. Walking. Pressing an intercom.

"Hello?"

Robert's voice? She found focus and stared at the name typed over the brass button. "Robert?"

"Don't move, Katie. I'm coming down."

Had he heard something in her voice? Kate blinked at the opening door, surprised to find the concern in his dark blue eyes.

"What did he do?"

Robert's hand closed around her upper arm and the contact jarred her. The reality of what Mack had been doing crashed in on her. How long? With Francesca? How long? Robert led her to the lift, asking no further questions. It was a blur, until Kate sat on a small sofa. He pressed a hot mug of tea into her numb hands. Sunlight spilled across the pale, wooden floor and Kate stared at the bright patterns. None of it felt real. The tea burned her throat and she put the cup down. Her hand trembled.

"Katie?"

Robert's solid presence on the seat beside her, an arm around her shoulders, calmed her. Kate leaned into his warmth, breathing in his familiar, reassuring scent. How did she begin to explain? She suspected that Robert had always had a soft spot for Francesca. Like most men. Pain clenched fist-tight in her stomach. "Francesca."

The hand stroking her hair stopped. "What about her?"

Kate closed her eyes. Oh, they were both fools. "I saw them."

"Katie, I'm sure—"

She pulled out of his hold, held his gaze. She swallowed past the lump in her throat. "She hugged him, kissed him." She let out a slow, shuddering breath. "I'm an idiot. I knew Fran was always dazzled by his wealth. And Mack could never resist a beautiful woman." Her eyes closed and the tear ran down her cheek. Her hasty finger wiped at the wetness. "I never knew Fran could do that to me."

She bit at the inside of her cheek to stop a further run of tears. The cruelty of her sister stabbed at her. And the money? Some nasty joke played by both of them? "Robert?"

There was something lost in his eyes. Kate had never truly realized. Francesca had always flirted with him, as she did with every man she met. But he'd been too polite and had never been rich enough. "Robert? Can I stay here for a few days?"

"Yes, of course."

She closed her hand around his, held it tight. "I'm sorry, I didn't know how you felt."

"Madness," he murmured. He let go of her hand with a half smile and pushed himself onto his feet. "She's driven me crazy."

"Francesca will do that to you."

The wry smile brought out his dimples. "We're a pair."

"Yes, yes we are."

ℇ

"Mackenzie." Mack fell back into the armchair, catching his breath after the dash for the telephone.

"Mr. Mackenzie—"

"Margaret?" His heart squeezed and he jerked upright. He couldn't keep the sudden fear from his voice. "Is everything all right? Kate. Is she—"

"She's gone, sir," said his housekeeper. "Left. Took her holdall. Got into a car with a tall, dark-haired gentleman."

A fierce anger burned away his fear. "Robert Thorpe."

"She did call him Robert, sir, yes."

Mack resisted the urge to curse. "How long?"

"The car's just pulled out of the drive."

"And she didn't say where she was going?"

"No, sir."

"Thank you, Margaret."

The line went dead and Mack tightened his fingers around the telephone. He itched to smash it against the far wall, watch it splinter into a thousand pieces. "The *hypocritical…*" He slammed the receiver back into its unit. The thought that she knew about Angela had burned through his mind, made him try to dampen his conscience with a large bottle of whiskey. But he had awoken that morning, his tongue like an old carpet and what he very reluctantly labeled guilt still tearing at him.

"Ours wasn't a real marriage." He blew out bad air. "And neither is this one."

For a brief, hate-filled second, he wanted to leave Kate where she was. Let her stew. But he had a responsibility to the baby she carried. That was the reason he grabbed the phone, rang Angela. Any finer feelings for Kate had died long ago. However, she had made a deal with him. Mack wanted an address on Robert Thorpe. Kate was *his* wife. He was about to remind her of that fact.

࡟

Kate curled into clean sheets. A bath had eased the tension from her muscles and Robert's very comfortable spare bed welcomed her body. She had scurried from the bathroom, but Robert had been dozing in an armchair, a book slipping out of his grasp. Smiling, she marked his place and put the book on the floor.

But now to find sleep, not to think. It was a relief to know that Mack didn't realize where she was hiding out. She needed this bolt hole.

She stretched her limbs under the light covers. "Thinking about it tomorrow." She pushed down the sour ache at the image seeping back into her mind. Seeing the slow kiss, the playful pull at his bottom lip.

"Damn it." Her body twisted away from the memory and purposefully Kate closed her eyes. Sleep, and no dreaming. A wry smile pulled at her mouth. "Doctor's orders."

A slamming door had her jumping awake. "Robert?" She struggled sleepily out of bed, reaching for her dressing gown.

"Where the hell is she?"

She had been tying the thin belt. She stared down at her hands and willed them to stop trembling. It didn't work. "Oh God."

The door burst open.

"Mack."

His cold fury found her and her insides clenched. Her hands grew bloodless around the stupid belt. Mack's gaze fixed on the warm and rumpled bed and something in him ignited. Kate backed away.

She had never seen him this angry. The taut lines of his body screamed it. Her escape had awoken something wild, primal. He kicked at the door. But Robert, his face grim, forced it open.

"You can't just burst in here—"

"I think I need a few minutes alone with my *wife*."

Kate saw the balled fists, the fury written plainly on every part of her husband. "Robert, please."

Her request made Mack's knuckles show white.

"If you're sure, Katie."

"She is." The door slammed. Mack's gaze fixed on the bed again and slid back to her. Kate inched away, wincing when the rough, exposed brick scraped her thin dressing gown. Mack was too close. "Did you think that I wouldn't find you?"

The warm scent of leather filled her, making her heart miss a beat. His heat washed over her but she shivered when his fingertips traced her jaw. Mack's dark brown eyes burned through her. Kate remembered to breathe.

"What is this, Kate? Taking the first opportunity to be with him?" His voice was hard.

Oh, one rule for him… Anger curled in her stomach. "I came to see you today."

His eyes narrowed, but there was no guilt. None.

"I saw you with my sister."

"Francesca."

"Yes, I only have one." Anger kept her on her feet, though her stomach growled for food and her head spun. Her hand pressed against Mack's jacket, wanting to push him away. However, her fingers slid over the soft, almost buttery leather. The memory of their very first kiss burned through her mind. She pulled her hand away. Kate fought to clear her thoughts, her emotions. "How long has *that* been going on?"

"Acting the concerned little wife?" No denial. Her insides ached. She jumped at the hands that gripped her arms. "Sit down, before you fall down." He pushed her onto the bed, the hard look on his face made her heart thud painfully. "What I do with Francesca has little to do with you."

Kate had to know how long he and her sister had been…together. She swallowed bile. Her heart cracked. Was this why Francesca had been shocked at their marriage? Tiredness swept over her and she covered her face with a shaking hand. She simply wanted to curl on her bed, sleep, and pretend none of it was real.

"However, what's happening *here* has a lot to do with *me*."

"I needed a place to think," she murmured.

"Did it worry you, someone else sharing my money?"

He was enjoying rubbing her nose in it. "I'm tired and I feel sick. Leave me alone, Mack."

"Get dressed, Kate. You're coming with me."

"Mack."

"You signed the pre-nuptial."

Kate let out a long, slow sigh. "My life has always been such a mess."

"All of your own making."

"Yes." Mack lifted her holdall onto the bed and Kate pulled clothes out, uncaring. She found his gaze on her. "Turn around."

"You keep having these fits of modesty," he said, presenting her with his broad back.

Kate slid the dressing gown from her shoulders and tugged the nightshirt over her head. She scrambled into her underwear before pulling on a light jersey top and long skirt. Her bare feet slipped into her sandals. Kate looked up to say she was ready to go and her cheeks flamed. She met Mack's searing gaze in the long mirror. Had he been watching her the entire time?

"Don't fret, Kate, it's nothing I haven't seen before."

That answered her question. "Pervert."

A hard grin cut his face. "Can't a man enjoy seeing his wife's body?"

The warmth in her cheeks flared. "Thanks, Mack. Make me feel like meat."

"My pleasure." He stuffed her nightwear into the holdall and jerked the zip around. "Is this everything?"

"There're some things still in the bathroom."

"Get them."

Kate snapped off a salute, but found her arm caught in Mack's strong fingers.

"I think you need another little reminder of where we stand."

"Mack—"

Blood burned under her skin and she forced herself to look at him. Mack stood too close. Again. His face was unreadable. Kate blinked when his finger slowly traced over her hot cheek. Even the slight touch sent a shock through her. Her hands balled into fists, reining in the desire to return his touch. He saw it as control, not mutual. She forced her breathing into an even rhythm.

"You want this." Mack's finger slipped across to explore the shell of her ear, eyes narrowing at the shiver he caused. "Want me." His dark eyes held her, scorched. One long finger delayed on her lips. Mack's face was harsh, his mouth set in a cruel line. "Want me to finish what we always start."

"It's been a long day, Mack," she said quietly. "I'll go with you. But I want to sleep. That's all."

Mack made her look at him, fingers firm on her jaw. There was still a bitter edge to his mouth. "Are you *sure* that's all?"

"Please stop this."

"Stop what, Kate?" He stroked a feather-like touch over her lip, a callous smile tugging at his mouth. His voice was smooth, silken. Another shiver ran over her skin. She should not be reacting to him. But it was Mack. The only man she had ever, would ever love. His voice was brittle. "Don't tell me that Thorpe could ever satisfy you."

"Don't."

His hands slid over her waist, her hips, pulling her body to him. She gasped at the close contact. "Tell me to stop, Kate." His lips brushed her neck, slow, soft, moving over her skin, a delicious ache that made her tremble.

There was no rushed passion, but a deliberate, controlled exploration of her ear, her throat, the line of her jaw. Kate closed her eyes against the burning torture. Her mind kept repeating that it was Mack trying to control her. That she should say stop.

Her hands clenched to bloodless fists, nails digging deep, but still, the words wouldn't come to her lips. Blood pounded at the burn of his lips on her skin. It was hard to breathe. She had to fight this need for him.

Mack's mouth captured hers and met no resistance, fierce, unforgiving, stoking the fire burning up through her body. She knew where the kiss would lead and the thought crushed her harder against him, thrusting her fingers under his shirt to the warm, smooth texture of his skin.

Mack pulled his mouth away, brushed his lips, his tongue, over her throat. Kate sighed against the shivery touch. "Don't stop," she whispered, hating herself for the weakness of that admission.

"See?"

The word penetrated her fused brain. His tone. He was laughing at her now, had proven how far he could push her. Kate staggered away from him. "Enough, Mack. You've had your fun now."

His dark eyes burned her. "Have I?"

The threat in his voice made her back away, wincing as the dressing table edge dug into her thighs. His look sent gooseflesh over her skin and she resisted the urge to run her tongue over dry lips. Kate could still feel the lean, hard pressure of his body imprinting hers. But she couldn't give into the desire to have him. Mack's eyes were hard, angry. It was all about power.

The door shook under a banging fist. "Katie? Are you all right?"

Mack lifted an eyebrow. "Your white knight?"

Kate melted at his touch. Always had. Always would. God, it was embarrassing. "I'm fine, Robert." She let out a slow breath and lifted reluctant eyes to meet Mack's. Still that cold burn. Her heart shriveled. "What else do you need to prove, Mack? I'm a pushover."

He tucked away a stray strand of hair, deliberately brushing the sensitive skin below her ear. She shivered involuntarily. "Yes, you are, aren't you?"

"Damn you."

Mack caught the fingers itching to slap his face. There was something in his eyes that Kate couldn't read. "Too late," he said.

•

Mack threw the holdall into the boot of his Audi and slammed it shut.

He drew in a lungful of fresh air and willed himself to be calm. The sharp edges of his fury still rattled through him. He hadn't expected that. Oh, he had been angry in his apartment but had calmed down as he waited for Angela to work her magic. The drive to Thorpe's pokey little flat had been relaxed. Theirs wasn't a real marriage, simply one of common sense.

Someone was leaving and he caught the main entrance door. Calm in the lift. Knowing that he would knock, ask to see Kate, explain the practicalities to her.

And then Thorpe had opened the door and he saw red and lost it.

Mack ran his fingers through his hair. It was simply a reaction to Francesca's unexpected petulance. Her huff over the dinner party had cut into his hangover. It had nothing to do with finding Thorpe, his clothes creased, his hair sticking up, and Kate undressed in a still-warm bed.

He climbed into the driving seat and slammed the door. He raked his gaze over Kate's profile as she stared at her hands, knotted in her lap. Her skin was almost translucent and there was a tremble to her lips. Damn it. Why could he still taste her? And how could any woman look so fragile and yet be made of rigid steel? The fragility was an act. That's what he had to remember the second time around.

"Is that everything you had at the house?"

Kate looked at him and blinked. "Yes."

"Saves me a trip. You're moving into the apartment."

"With you?"

Mack started up the engine and pulled away from the kerb. "I can't trust you, Kate, can't leave you alone for a minute. And the apartment's more convenient for the office."

Her attention was back on the road. "Then shouldn't we set up some rules?"

"Such as?"

"No entertaining."

The hard smile pulled at his mouth. "Ah, 'entertaining'. A strange request since it's obviously more of a hardship for you than for me." Kate bristled, anger spiking off her. "But then we always have each other."

"I have no desire—"

Mack's gaze caught hers as it sparked with blue fire. "Pregnancy does stunt your memory, doesn't it?" He watched the flush rise under her pale cheeks. "Additional to the first rule, you are to cut Thorpe out of your life."

"Don't be ridiculous. I work with the man."

"We've already had that discussion. I've bought you, Kate."

"Like you buy everyone," she muttered. "Like you bought my sister."

"I'm not discussing Francesca with you."

She turned her face to the passenger window. "No, no, of course you're not."

Mack's gaze slid over the pale column of her throat, the soft curve of her collarbone. The memory of the salt-sweet taste of her skin burned through him. Angered at his lapse, he stared at the traffic light, willing it to change. It was insane to still want her. Francesca was a more worthy woman.

The light changed to green. Tires squealed as he tore away from the lights.

Chapter Eight

Kate stared at herself in the long mirror. What was she doing, agreeing to this farce?

Her fingers slid down the soft flow of her new dress. The fabric clung to her curves, the soft swell of her abdomen, fell in a smooth rush to her feet. She traced over the thin shoulder strap, wishing that she didn't love the expensive gown, that the color, a rich plum, didn't complement her skin tone, adding a life, a warmth, that had been lacking for too many weeks.

Mack had stood over her in the small, exclusive boutique, impersonally tugging and pulling the delicate fabric around her body as if she'd been a mannequin. It made her feel like a piece of meat. Which, she was sure, was his plan.

But she hadn't expected the stylist. A woman who made her glow with clever touches of makeup, made her hair fall around her shoulders like a bolt of dark silk. Mack was simply making certain that the arm ornament, for which he had paid, looked suitably good in front of his high-powered friends.

"What do I know about dinner parties?" She fiddled with the fine, white-gold chain, the small cluster of diamonds. "Put on the work face. That'll have to get me through this."

"The first car's pulled up." Mack entered her room without knocking. His gaze slid up and down her body, judging her like a prize heifer. Kate felt sick. "Marie did a good job, as always."

She blinked. "As always?"

"These parties have to have a hostess, Kate," he said. He straightened his bowtie in her mirror. "For the past year, it's been Francesca."

Blood drained from her face. Her stomach turned. It had been five days since she had caught her sister with Mack. Five days in which she *couldn't* contact Francesca. She didn't want to know the true depth of her betrayal. But Mack wanted to rub her face in it.

She took a steadying breath. The dinner party had now spiralled into a nightmare. The guests had no doubt already met Francesca and would begin comparing. She flicked a glance back to the mirror, all joy in her appearance evaporating. Being the short, ugly, studious sister, she had little chance against Francesca's model height and looks. Kate didn't have the ability to switch on the charm, to flirt and flatter.

"Why didn't you ask her tonight?" She backed away from her disappointing reflection.

"You're my wife, Kate."

"Yes. How could I forget that?" She straightened her spine. "You said the first car's arrived. Shouldn't we...?" She waved to the closed door.

"We're supposed to be newlyweds." A warm fingertip caressed her collarbone, making her gasp. "Don't be horrified if I behave like a besotted husband. My guests expect it."

Kate edged away from his touch. She questioned again how she could love this man. Was she in love with the man she thought he once was? But it did hurt. To look at him, to think of him, to feel his touch.

It seared through her, carrying the knowledge that he didn't even try to like her in return.

Kate let out a slow breath. "Let's go down," she said. "Get this over with."

"Remember to smile." His gaze held her, cold, hard. "And nothing about the baby this time."

Francesca wouldn't have needed to be coached. Her sister could sparkle on demand. "Yes," she muttered.

Mack held dinner parties at his house, never the apartment. That reminder floated through her brain as Kate descended the broad staircase to the elegant marble-floored entrance. She slid her fingers over the mahogany rail. They tightened when a sense of déjà vu rushed her. Too much like his grandfather's Regimental Dinner. It filled her with a sudden foreboding.

Margaret met them at the bottom of the stairs. She rattled off a list of things to which Kate paid little attention. She wasn't supposed to. Margaret directed all conversation to Mack.

The paneled front doors opened to admit a tall, grey-haired man and a long-legged blonde woman less than half his age. Kate remembered her stitched-on smile, but it wavered as Mack rested warm fingers on her hip.

"Mack. Heard you got hitched. 'Bout time you and— Oh." The man stopped, stared. He winced and his gaze dropped away from Kate. "Heard it was someone else." He held out a meaty hand to Kate. "Andy Beaumont. This is Leah Wilson."

Kate's fingers lost themselves in Andy's heavy grip. "Kate Hartley."

Andy blinked and Leah stared. "Any relation to Francesca Hartley?"

Kate heard the surprise in his voice. But she knew it was the question that had to come. This was simply the first time. "Sister."

Andy stared at Mack. "Really?"

"Come through for a drink, Andy. You've had a long drive."

Leah dropped into step beside her, smiling a bright, open smile. Kate's nerves eased.

"Known Mack long?"

"A number of years," Kate said. He hadn't coached her on whether she could reveal that they'd been married before. If she should try to explain why *she* hadn't helped to host Mack's parties... It made her feel gauche, stupid. "We met up again and..." She shrugged.

Leah's gaze settled on Andy, clinking glasses with Mack. Her smile grew. "...it felt right."

Kate ignored the stab of envy at the shine of love in Leah's eyes. "Something like that," she said.

The other guests soon arrived. Kate smiled and social kissed her way through the eight people who appeared shortly after Andy and Leah. Her jaw muscles ached, but the raw rush of fear had ebbed. Mack's friends seemed surprised that he hadn't married "someone else". But after their initial unease, everyone was polite, friendly, even welcoming.

Kate sipped at her drink, letting the cool mineral water ease her throat, and watched the interaction of people who knew each other too well. Of course, she knew who they believed Mack had married. She willed herself to breathe past the flare of pain. And she'd thought that Angela Craven had been her rival. Never her sister—

The soft clinking of a spoon against crystal made her look up.

"Well, it seems that Jonathon is late," Mack began.

"Again," Andy said and was greeted with knowing laughter.

"So we should go through."

Mack caught her eye, a smile briefly curving his mouth. She knew she had to fall in with Mack's act. This, as he kept reminding her, was what she had signed up for. She would go into the dining room on his arm and maintain the pretense. Act the good little wife and hostess. Just the dinner to get through now. Not so difficult—

The front doors slammed. "Sorry I'm late," a tall, dark-haired man declared, shedding his outer coat into the waiting hands of the butler. "But you know how impossible some women can be."

"Jonathon!"

Her laughing voice.

Kate felt all eyes on her. Heat crept up her face. A knot pulled tight in her stomach. Oh no. She jumped at the warm fingers that closed over her shoulder.

"Mack, Kate, congratulations!" Kate found herself enveloped in a too tight hug, one she didn't return. Mack's secure touch vanished.

"Francesca."

Kate heard the thread of fury in his voice. Was he upset that his wife and his mistress were in the same house?

"Mack."

Francesca's long, bare arm slipped through his with familiar ease. The dazzling smile lit her face. Her head rested briefly on his shoulder and Kate saw the edge of his anger die. It brought a pained lump to her throat. Did he…? But she couldn't think the word. If she did, she wouldn't be able to stay in the same room.

Francesca was talking again, her voice light, teasing. "It's time to eat. I'm starving!"

A man's fingers pried the glass from her hand and put her arm through his. "I'm Jonathon Kane," he said in a smooth, smiling voice.

But his pale blue eyes were hard. Sickened, Kate wondered what lies Francesca had woven around this man. "And I offer my congratulations."

He stared at her abdomen and then looked up. A brief flash of dislike burned through her. Kate made the smile grow on her mouth, hoping that her face hadn't betrayed her. For a second, she wondered where she had gone wrong with Francesca, why her sister seemed to delight in hurting her. "Thank you, Jonathon," she said, clinging to her manners. "Mack and I are very happy to have found each other again."

The man blinked. So, Francesca hadn't told him everything. She was slipping. But, as Kate was discovering, her sister's life seemed to be a tangled web of lies. It had to be difficult to keep track. "Shall we go through?"

Kate watched her sister sashay into the grand dining room. The scrap of red silk that constituted her dress displayed Francesca's endless, tanned legs. Her hair a loose bolt of shining black, flowed with the slow, inviting movement of her hips. Francesca knew how beautiful she was—knew it and flaunted it. Kate wanted to hate her, hate her for the burning pain that scorched her heart, but stupidly she still loved her sister. And then the horrifying thought struck her and she practically fell into the chair Jonathon held out for her.

What if it was more than his money? Mack pulled out the chair for Francesca, seating her to his right. Her sister smiled her thanks and there was something in the softness of his smile that made Kate close her eyes. It wasn't a "what if". Francesca loved him. All the lies had been a fight for the man she loved.

Jonathon had already poured her a fresh glass of mineral water and Kate's numb fingers picked it up, swallowing automatically. She wanted to run, run into the night and keep on running. Mack's gaze cut into her blank stare. He looked beautiful in the soft light, a flicker of gold in his dark eyes. But the rest of his face was hard, unsmiling. She saw his eyes narrow and she had to fight the sudden compulsion to kick back her chair and escape.

Kate twitched a smile across her mouth instead and put the glass back on the table with deliberate care. She breathed in, breathed out. She fixed on the glow of the candles, the way their light caught on the old, silver cutlery, on the array of crystal glasses set before each place. The delicate scent of summer flowers soothed her pounding heart. She had to stay calm.

Kate almost jumped at the server, who silently placed her starter before her. She smiled briefly at the man, knowing that Francesca would be served at the same time. A sour thought ran in her mind. Had her sister deliberately targeted Jonathon, knowing, intimately, the arrangement of Mack's dinner parties, that Jonathon Kane's guest always sat to the right of Mack? But such scheming…

Automatic fingers picked up her cutlery. Her stomach was growling. However, there was a taste of bile in her throat and she doubted that she could swallow anything. She resisted the urge to poke at the black olives, the slivers of mozzarella on bruschetta. It smelled beautiful, with hints of pepper, of marjoram. Think about the food. Think about trying to have a normal conversation with the people around her. Francesca's laugh cut through her calm. Soft, throaty, sensual. Mack's followed it. Kate's hand tightened around her knife and the warmed handle dug into her palm. It was going to be a long night.

And after the meal, she would speak to Francesca. She had to.

❧

Taking a silent cue from Mack, Kate rose stiffly to her feet. "There's coffee waiting for us in the drawing room."

"Hopefully the filter worked this time."

Remembered laughter followed Francesca's words. Kate caught her sister's eye and saw the look of victory. The rich food soured in her stomach but she forced a smile on to her mouth. "I've been personally assured that it's perfect. Or they'll rip up the bill."

"Here's hoping for sludge then," Andy said.

Kate led the way into the drawing room, opening the heavy double doors on to the softly lit room. The day had been warm, but the night was chilly and Margaret had lit a fire in the large hearth. Tendrils of heat licked at her legs and Kate sipped at her coffee. Francesca slid onto the long couch, patting the seat beside her for Mack. Only a little while longer, Kate told herself. Then she could have a private conversation with her sister.

One by one, the guests either left or retired to the rooms they normally occupied. Kate knew her chance was coming and climbed onto tired feet. It was past midnight and she was feeling the late hour, but— "Francesca?" Good. Her voice was strong, not quavering with the panic that made her heart pound. "Could you help me take these cups through to the kitchen?"

"Margaret will get them," Francesca said.

"Margaret went to bed over an hour ago."

Francesca shrugged. "The caterers should be back in the morning—"

"Fran!" The laziness threw Kate back to the flat they had shared for too many years.

Francesca let out a slow sigh. "Everything always has to be how you want it." She stood and straightened her silk dress over her thighs. "You stack, I'll carry."

"They do come back in the morning to clear and tidy," Mack murmured as he helped to put cups on the tray. "You don't have to."

"I do."

His dark eyes held her, softened by the embers of the dying fire, the golden glow of the lamps. She wanted to think that there was something there for her, but Mack had the sweet scent of brandy on his breath. Fine alcohol had made him mellow.

"I hated being a waitress," Francesca said, lifting the tray.

"You only lasted half a day," Jonathon objected.

"See? Hated it."

Kate closed the door on the laughter. Silently they walked through the labyrinth of corridors to the kitchen. Kate flicked on the lights and headed for the sink. She needed to be occupied, not to stand in front of her sister with wringing hands. Warm, soapy water splashed into the first coffee pot.

"Are you going to bite my head off?" Francesca asked, dumping the tray on to the large kitchen table.

Kate scrubbed at the insides of the ceramic pot. Now that Francesca was here, ready to be interrogated, fear seized her. She didn't want to know.

"Look." Francesca flopped into a chair and absently stretched her spine. "This has all turned into one big mess. I shouldn't have turned up tonight. That was bad, inconsiderate of me." She let out a sigh. "I've already apologized to Mack about five thousand times."

"How long?" Kate set the first pot on the drainer and started attacking another. She couldn't turn around.

"How long what?"

"Mack."

"Oh him."

Kate heard the lazy smile in her sister's voice and her hand tightened around the wet cloth.

"Long time." Francesca's thoughtful little sigh set Kate's teeth on edge. "He's always been fascinated with me."

Francesca had been drinking. Kate wondered whether she was forgetting to whom she was talking. Or did she know? Exactly.

"That seems to happen to men. They can't help it. *I* can't help it."

Kate let out a slow breath, stared down at the dirty water in the deep Belfast sink. She had to ask, yet the words wouldn't come. She bit at her lip before asking, "How...how," she silently cursed her stammer, "do you...think...of him?"

"How do I think of Sean Mackenzie?" There was something in her voice. Damn her, she thought this was funny. "You have to admit, Kate, he is one of the most gorgeous men you've ever seen. Even Robert—" She cut off the rest of her words. Her voice changed, hard, determined. "In the beginning, it was his money. I had that *big* credit problem and you were a student, sinking into debt."

Francesca's words burned. Kate had thought it would be a recent meeting, but her sister was talking over five years. Five years. And Mack had bought Francesca, making a mockery of what he thought of *her*. Cold words erupted and she turned to her sister. "You were a big part of that debt, Fran. You still are."

"Kate!"

"You're very good at spending money." She should have made Francesca stand on her own two feet years before. "You bled us both."

"I needed the cash. You divorced a multi-millionaire over some slight—"

"He accused me of whoring myself for his money."

"Well, you were the one who said you'd bagged the man of the century."

Kate stared at her sister. It had been a joke, said to her friends when they asked her about Mack, about his money. "You told him."

A steeled look entered her features. "You said that I wouldn't see any of his money. It's not my fault he took it that way."

Kate sank into a chair. "How could you, Francesca?"

"Anyway, this is academic." Francesca pushed herself on to her feet, brushing at her dress with careful fingers. "I said his money mattered in the beginning. Mack and I have been together a long time, Kate." Cold blue eyes fixed on her. "*You're* an aberration." Her gaze slid to her abdomen. "An obligation."

"Get out."

"With pleasure."

"Out of this house. Now."

"You can't—"

"I'm Mack's wife, this is *my* home." Kate stood. "And as of today, *neither* of us will bankroll you."

"Mack won't refuse me anything. And he certainly won't force me out of his house tonight." A smile cut her red lips. "I think I'll tell him right now." She turned to leave.

"Does he know you conned money from *both* of us?"

Francesca stopped.

"I thought not." A headache had started to pound at the edges of her skull. It was too much to have Francesca in the same house; to think that later in the night Mack might sneak— "Jonathon doesn't drink. Tell him you've forgotten about an early morning appointment." Kate choked back a harsh laugh. "Make him believe that *you* could do early mornings."

"You haven't won, Kate." Francesca tossed back her thick hair. "I love Mack." The superior smile. "And Mack loves me. It's been that way for a long time."

"Just get out, Francesca."

"This isn't over—"

"What part of 'get out' did you not understand?"

She winced as Francesca slammed the kitchen door.

ⅎ

Kate scrubbed the cold cream into her skin, wanting to remove all evidence of makeup. Francesca was the little painted doll. Not her. She attacked her hair with a stiff brush. "*I love Mack. And Mack loves me.*" The words seared through her brain and the brush clattered to the floor. Her chest tightened, her eyes burning with unshed tears.

But she had vowed not to cry. She had cried enough for one lifetime.

She stared at her pale skin, still sallow from tiredness and nausea. Francesca had started the trouble that crushed her marriage. The action of a spite-filled child. But Mack had believed her. That said everything about their too hasty vows.

Kate remembered the slam of the apartment door, the angry stride over wooden floors. She had been writing an essay in the study, hadn't expected her husband home for hours. Kate closed her eyes. The burning ache never seemed to fade.

"*Mack.*" *She stopped at the doorway to the study, the words frozen in her mouth. His dark eyes were cold, icy black chips of hatred. She swallowed.* "*What's…what's the matter? What's happened?*"

"*Infatuated?*" *he grated.* "*Love-struck?*"

"*What?*"

"*Using that infatuation,*" *his hard voice sneered the word,* "*to grab cash?*"

"*Mack—*"

"*The last thing I ever thought you were was a whore, Kate.*"

"*Excuse me?*"

"*A whore?*"

Kate backed away, hissing as the edge of her desk caught her legs.

"*Definition—woman who has sex with a man for money.*" *His smile cut his features and she shivered* "*Sound like you?*"

"*No.*" *Heat shot through her face.* "*I have never—*"

"*Large withdrawals have been made from your account, Kate.*"

She stared. "*But that's private information.*"

"*You're running through money like water. Where's the necklace I gave you, the bracelet?*"

"*In their boxes, in the bedroom,*" *she said, pushing past him. She scrambled through drawers, but there was nothing. The last thing she remembered doing with them was showing…* "*Francesca. She must have borrowed them.*"

"*Francesca?*"

Kate caught her fingers in her hair, trying to think, trying to understand why he was making such horrible accusations. "*Yes.*" *She stared at the open drawer, almost willing the velvet-lined boxes to reappear. She had never owned anything as beautiful as those pieces of jewelry. Yet even if they had been ugly paste, she would have loved them. They were a gift from Mack.* "*When she gets back from school—*"

"*You won't be here.*"

"*What?*"

"*You used me, Kate. I don't forget and I don't forgive.*"

"*You're throwing me out?*"

"*I'm divorcing you.*"

The bottom fell out of her heart. She couldn't breathe and sank into a nearby chair. Mack lifted her chin, fingers warm against her skin. She wanted him to say that he hadn't meant it, that there'd obviously been a huge mistake.

"*Tears? Do I have to pay for them, too?*"

Kate bit back a sob. She was crumbling, falling apart. Mack didn't love her anymore.

"*Keep your money,*" *she grated.* "*I hope you rot in it.*"

She moved, threw clothes into a suitcase. Mack stood and glared. Did he think she'd try to steal one of the pricey little trinkets littering the apartment? She would talk to him when he'd calmed down, but until then she would escape to her mother's home. Sentiment had found her unable to part with the tiny flat.

"Now I've even lost that." Kate stared at her face in the mirror, at the wet run of her tears.

The door to the bedroom thudded open and the landing light framed Mack there. Kate wiped quickly at her wet face. Mack sat on the end of her bed. He had lost his dinner jacket and his tie hung loose around his neck. The top button of his dress shirt was undone, revealing more of his smooth, brown skin. It made the breath catch in Kate's throat, that and his subtle, spiced scent.

His gaze clashed with hers in the mirror. "What did you say to Francesca?"

"It's after one, Mack. I'm tired." She couldn't look at him. He loved her sister. Had he imagined her face, her body when they'd...

Kate put her hand to her mouth and breathed past the sudden nausea. "Really. You should go."

"I'm not going anywhere tonight."

"What?"

"I told you in the beginning, I have a reputation to uphold. How would it look? Newly married and sleeping in separate bedrooms?"

"Maybe they'll think that your wife threw you out because your friend invited your mistress."

Mack suddenly looked tired. "God, Kate, is there anyone you think I *haven't* slept with?"

"Within your immediate circle? No." Kate climbed on to weary feet. Her headache was back and she didn't want to discuss Francesca, not when the wound was still fresh. "Mack, I'm not fit for our usual fight. Can you let me sleep?"

"Do you think I can't resist your charms? Is that it?"

Another barb. Silently, she slipped her dressing gown down her shoulders and laid it over a nearby chair. She tried to ignore the man sitting at the end of her bed and pulled back the bedcovers. The sheets were cold. Kate curled into ball, pulling her nightshirt around her knees. She wanted him to leave, but an insane part of her wanted him to stay, to put strong arms around her and tell her that Francesca meant nothing.

The mattress creaked. In the quietness of the room, Kate heard the slide of buttons through starched cloth, the metal pull of a zip. Her heart was in her throat and it was stupid. Mack cared about her insofar as she was carrying his child. There was nothing beyond that. The dinner and Francesca's acid words had proven it.

The bed dipped and Kate held tight to her sheet, to the soft wool of the blankets. The heat of his bare flesh tantalized her. She fought the temptation to inch back into his warmth, to know that it was Mack surrounding, protecting her. Hurt and guilt warred within her. It wasn't right that she should love him. Not anymore.

"Kate?"

His voice was close. Had she imagined the brush of his breath over her ear?

"I didn't know Francesca was coming tonight. She knew—"

"It's a mistake to get on her wrong side," Kate interrupted. She let out a slow sigh. "She plays dirty."

There was a smile in his voice and Kate's chest tightened. "As I'm discovering."

Kate's mind raced with how she could bring up the subject of Francesca's "allowance". Mack had to curb her spending. Was probably the only one who could anymore. She had been a spectacular failure. "How much did you pay Francesca for hosting these dinner parties?" Kate stared into the darkness and concentrated on keeping her breathing even. But her heart pounded.

"Kate."

She heard the warning in his voice. She wanted to turn, see the anger in his eyes and soothe it away with gentle fingers. "She's twenty-three and has no sense with money."

"A genetic failing?"

She took a steadying breath and decided to build on his opinion. "I've failed her. She also spends to excess, gives it no thought. Only you have—" Her words and courage died. She couldn't state what they *did* share. That knowledge was still too raw.

"Making her accountable?" The mattress creaked again and she felt the heat of him, almost pressed against her back. She swallowed in a dry throat. "Kate, I need to tell—"

"Go to sleep, Mack." She prayed he hadn't heard the panic in her voice. She didn't want him to confirm his relationship with Francesca. She had tried. Kate jumped as his large hand brushed a slow caress over her hip. Then his touch was gone. She would not cry. She wouldn't.

"Good night," he murmured.

Kate closed her eyes, knowing sleep would never find her that night. Surely, it wouldn't get any worse. A wry smile lifted her lips. She kept thinking that but something new would steam right over her. But she had to be right this time, didn't she?

Chapter Nine

Laughter. It stopped Kate at the doorway to Mack's office. There was something free about the sound. A strange guilt consumed her when she realized that he sounded happy. Her throat tightened and tears burned. She had brought chaos to his life with an unexpected pregnancy, when he had never wanted children.

She almost walked away, destined never to tell him about her hospital appointment. But their child deserved to have him involved. Kate took a deep breath and pushed open the wide door. There was a burst of mechanical whirring and she yelped as a large, remote-control car crashed into her feet.

A little boy ran to retrieve it. Kate stared. He could be no more than five years old with a shock of sandy-gold hair. His cheeks were flushed, a wide grin on his small face as he looked up at her. His eyes. An intense and shining dark brown.

Distantly, Kate heard a woman laughing. "Jason, be careful! Sorry, he's a handful—" A pause. "Oh, it's you."

Angela. Everything slowed and Kate stared at the woman walking toward her. Saw the smile slip from her face and replaced with a hard dislike. Protective hands closed over Jason's shoulders and guided him from her path.

"We'd better be going." Angela smiled down at her son, a hand moving to ruffle his untidy hair. "Thank Uncle Mack for the present, Jason."

The boy ran to Mack and threw his arms around his neck with a familiarity that pierced Kate's heart. "Thank you, Uncle Mack."

Kate stepped aside as they left. Words wouldn't come. Was she jumping to conclusions? But Jason's eyes, they were so like Mack's eyes.

"To what do I owe this honor?" The man broke into her thoughts. She looked up. The smile had gone from his face and he sat behind his desk, scanning papers.

Kate had woken up Sunday morning with Mack already gone from the bed, the sheet cold to the touch. There were vague memories of being wrapped in strong arms, feeling the security and warmth of a lean, hard body. But it had been a dream. It always would be. She'd decided to confront him with her decision about her job while she lay alone in the early morning darkness.

And why would he be concerned about the scan of yet another child? No. Work. She needed to be occupied. To have her nights filled with essays and prepping for seminars and lectures, not think about whose bed he was in. Pain shot through her. Her life was a total mess. Words tumbled out. "I'm going back to work."

"Like hell you are."

"I refuse to sit in that apartment and watch my stomach expand."

"That's what you signed up for."

"Did you do this to her?" The words were out and she instantly regretted them.

His eyes narrowed. "Who?"

"Never mind."

"Who, Kate?"

"*Her.*" Kate couldn't help the rush of anger. She hoped it didn't sound like jealousy.

"Angela?"

"Angela," she said with a grim smile. "Did you keep her away from the office for the entire pregnancy?"

"She had little choice."

He made her sick. "It's a wonder you let me wear shoes."

"Excuse me?"

Her head snapped up. "Barefoot and pregnant. Isn't that the expression? Is that how you like your women?" His expression remained hard. "Jason?" Her nails dug, sharp, into her palms to try to counteract the agony in her heart. "He's yours, isn't he?"

Mack stared. "What?"

"Jason, Angela's little boy."

Fire lit his gaze. "Here we go again," he grated. He rose from her chair. There was something slow, almost predatory to his movements. Kate's heart skipped a beat and she had to remember to breathe.

"It's a legitimate question, Mack."

"It was more like a statement." Only a few feet from her and Kate resisted the very strong urge to bolt. "You keep making these judgments, Kate. I'm a rapacious, sexual predator, fathering children left and right.

"I make judgments on what I see, on what I'm *told*, Mack," she said, unwilling to show the panic building in her.

His fingers stroked the edge of her jaw and shivers ran through her skin. But there was still the feverish burn to his eyes. "Strange, that you keep inventing women, when you obviously want me yourself."

His touch scorched down her neck, tugged aside the obscuring collar. The other hand invaded the warmth of her jacket, found the curve of her hip. She pressed against him, knowing only the roar of her blood, the pulsing ache low in her belly. She crushed her eyes against the need to taste the exposed skin of his throat, to let her tongue explore him. She should stop. But this was Mack. They both knew she would melt.

She had to answer him, deny it. "I've never invented anyone." Kate wanted to sound indignant, but his searching fingers had breached the band of her skirt and found the soft curve of her buttock. She gasped as his lips traced the sensitive skin below her jaw.

His harsh, whispered words against her flesh burned her. "Does it turn you on, thinking that all these phantom women want me?"

"No." Kate pulled back, her skin flushing. "It was a bad idea to come here."

Mack blocked her leaving with his body, caught her in strong hands. "Why did you?"

"Certainly not to meet your son." Kate struggled free. She saw his hands tighten into bloodless fists. Her gaze lifted, locked onto his. "Well, you haven't denied it, Mack."

"Angela met Mike Ashbury six years ago." His voice was low, controlled. "He's Jason's father."

The flush rose over her cheeks. "He has your eyes."

"He has *Angela's* eyes." She could still hear the grate of anger in his voice. "But you enjoy believing the worst of me."

She let out a slow sigh, not wanting this conversation. That would take her into feelings and she couldn't let him know how she felt. He was already in love, in a relationship with Francesca. Exposing herself to his mocking smile, hearing him detail their relationship. No. Time to change from one awkward subject to another. "I came about the scan," she said, her words rushed. She stepped back from him. "It's in two weeks, scheduled on my day off."

"You are not going back to work."

Kate ignored him. "The scan." She had to get it over with. Ask him, accept the rejection, get back to the apartment. "It's my first hospital appointment."

"Hospital?" The word seemed to break through the anger. But there was something else in his eyes that made her take another nervous back step.

"Blood tests, ultrasound, writing up notes about the mother, the father." She was rambling and she knew it, but his staring, his silence, made her jumpy.

"And you don't want me there, is that it?"

Kate blinked. He *wanted* to go?

"I've bought this baby, Kate."

Her heart sank. Obligation. She heard Francesca saying that word, heard the sneer in her sister's voice. "Yes." She wanted to escape. The deed was done. Mack knew about the scan, would go with her. The thought didn't fill her with joy, only the image of him watching a commodity on a screen. "I have to go."

"Damn it, Kate." She jerked to a stop when he grabbed her arm. "We have to sort out our relationship before the baby arrives."

"We don't have a relationship." She wanted to add the words, "You have that with someone else". But there was the fire in his eyes, the one she had to avoid for her own sanity. It promised passion, all-consuming. Throwing herself into it would leave her heart in ashes and Mack still in love with Francesca. "We have a business agreement." A bleak smile. "Or disagreement."

"Then consider this a form of conflict resolution."

So fast. Kate didn't have time to think, to protest. His mouth was on hers, demanding entrance. No tenderness. A scorching kiss that left her dazed, barely able to breathe, yet it couldn't stop, she wouldn't allow it. He was lifting her, the cool wood of the desk brushing her thighs. Mack insinuated himself between her legs, rubbing his hardness against her. Kate moaned deep in her throat, instinct arching her to meet him.

Mack's mouth ripped from hers. "You want me," he grated.

The heat of his skin, the sweet taste of him on her lips. It was wrong. He was her sister's lover— Kate couldn't look at the fingers that ran along her bared leg, shivering at callused thumbs on the sensitive skin of her inner thigh. His words penetrated the haze. "Yes," she sighed, and hated her own weakness. "Yes."

"Open your eyes."

Kate obeyed. Eyes black with desire held hers. Afternoon sunlight dappled his features with gold, her fingers, of their own bidding, tracing the patterns over his warm skin. She wanted to tell him that he was beautiful, that she loved him, find his mouth and show him.

The rapid patter of knocks on the door shocked awareness into Kate. She stared at the door, trying to control her breathing, push away the unfulfilled ache. She glanced down at her skirt. Blood baked under her skin when she found the loose material bunched around her upper thighs. Hastily, she pulled at it and struggled down from Mack's desk. She escaped to the wide windows.

Mack smoothed his fingers casually over his disheveled hair. "Come in."

There was nothing in his voice, no remnants of their wild burst of desire. Kate stared down at the city far below. Her heart pounded, her body tight with need. But to Mack it was another lesson, proof that he could bend her to his will. Bring her to heel. She winced against that unwanted image.

"Oh look, that's why. The receiver's off the cradle."

More embarrassment burned through Kate as Mack's assistant pointed out the disrupted desk, the messed files, laptop askew, the telephone receiver almost dangling.

"It's a Mr. Reeves, for you Mack," the assistant continued. "He says it's urgent."

"Put him through."

Now was the time to leave, Kate realized. She turned to the door.

"What about my mother?"

Kate stopped. Anger and fear reverberated through his voice.

"Out with it, man." She turned and caught the color draining from his face and heard the whispered word, "Found?" He seemed to sag in his chair. "Is she?" There was a bleakness to Mack's voice that tore at Kate's heart. Her own eyes filled with tears.

Mack's fingers slipped from the receiver, letting it fall to the desk.

"Mack?" Kate stepped forward, reaching out to touch his shoulder. He flinched. "What's happened?"

He closed his eyes. "My mother was repairing her stupid bloody roof. She fell."

Kate's heart contracted. "Is she all right?"

Mack shrugged and she knew he was struggling to comprehend. Without thinking, she slipped her arms around his shoulders and gently held him to her breast, fingers stroking over his hair. She breathed slowly, wanting to comfort him with the even beat of her heart. His arms tightened around her and she felt his fight to control his emotions, to control the fear.

"Is she in hospital?"

"Reeves said an estate worker found her. Phoned an ambulance." His arms constricted and she heard the hatred in his muffled voice. "The Colonel hasn't 'enquired further'. I don't even know where she was taken."

His arms slid back and he straightened in his chair. Mack was in control again. He probably hated her even more because she'd witnessed a moment of weakness.

"I need to get up there," he muttered. "Now."

&

Kate wondered whether Mack knew she was there.

She tagged behind him as he strode the fluorescent-bright corridors. The only information that he'd been able to glean, after his staff had found the hospital, was that his mother was stable. And Kate wasn't exactly sure why she had accompanied him, or why he'd let her. He would want Francesca. To see her draped over him—

Kate cut out that thought. It had no place in her head, not right now. Beth was hurt, perhaps badly. Another unwanted, unpleasant thought burst into her brain. What if his mother could no longer live at her cottage? Any deal struck with his grandfather would be void. Would that mean dissolving their charade of a marriage?

Mack disappeared through a side door, letting it slide back into place. Kate hesitated. She pressed her fingers to the cold glass. There was a single bed, hooked up to an alarming array of machines. Bright lights illuminated Beth's limp golden hair, a sharp contrast to the deep bruising on her face. A cage protected her chest and her left leg was raised and cast in plaster.

Kate watched Mack take his mother's hand, his focus fixed on the unconscious woman's face.

"You're here to see Mrs. Mackenzie?"

Kate jumped at the light touch on her shoulder. "Yes, I'm," the need to identify herself made her pause, "I'm her daughter-in-law."

"She's a very lucky lady," the nurse said, opening the door and waiting for her to enter. Reluctantly, Kate stepped into the room. "I'll tell the doctor you're here."

Kate bit at her lip, wishing the nurse hadn't left the room. Mack didn't acknowledge her, had probably forgotten she was there at all. She wanted to break the tense atmosphere, the silence broken only by the soft beeping of various machines. But trite reassurances lodged in her throat. Instead, she moved to the window, staring out at the neat rockery and burst of bright green shrubs.

"Mack?"

Mack turned to the door. A tall man in a neat, dark suit stood in the doorway. There was a friendly smile on his face.

He stared. Blinked. "James Roby?"

"The same." He unclipped the board from the end of the bed and scanned the attached sheets. "I thought it could be your mother," he said. He looked up, his face serious. "She's been very lucky, Mack."

Mack's gaze darted back to the bed and the fear lurched in his heart all over again. "Lucky?" He heard the disbelief in his voice and realized he was speaking. "She looks as if she's been hit by a train."

"You know she fell from a ladder? Well, she was lucky to land on grass and earth. She has a mild concussion, dislocated shoulder, three cracked ribs and a tibial fracture."

"That's lucky?" Mack barked.

"It sounds bad," James said with a wry smile. "But there're no internal injuries and minimal blood loss." He clipped the board back into place. "Your mother will make a full recovery, simply needing a period of therapy for her leg. A two story fall could've been much worse."

"How long will she have to stay here?"

"I'd give her another forty-eight hours. Minimum."

Mack let out a slow breath and his body sagged. His fingers slid through his untidy hair. His mother was alive and would recover. Only minutes before he had feared the worst. "Thanks, James."

"Aren't you going to introduce us?"

Mack blinked. He stared around the room and found Kate. What the hell? Where had she come from? Had she been on the flight with him? In his car? His brain kicked in. "Of course," he said. "Kate, this is James Roby. We were at school together. James, this is my wife, Kate Hartley."

Kate dutifully shook his hand and murmured pleasantries.

"You both look shattered, you should get some rest."

"I'd rather—"

"Your mother will be awake and making sense in the morning."

Mack gently squeezed the hand that lay outside of the blankets and moved away from his mother's bedside. "I'll be here first thing."

"I don't doubt it."

"Kate?" He caught her surprise as he put out his hand. Her fingers were cold and small in his and he couldn't help the little squeeze he gave her. "We'll stay at the Lodge." His gaze moved involuntarily back to the bed. His mother suddenly looked old, almost every day of her fifty-six years, and it hurt. He could have lost her. "She'd want to know someone was looking after the place."

The car was waiting outside. The journey back to the Colonel's estate was silent. Mack couldn't watch the houses, the countryside flash past, without thinking that only hours before an ambulance had rushed his mother to hospital.

It was almost twilight when they reached the Lodge. Mack was thankful that the growing gloom stopped him from searching for the patch of grass which had cushioned Beth's fall. The Lodge was in darkness. He found his keys and let himself into the silent cottage. He flicked on a light and saw the narrow hallway and twisting staircase with new eyes. "Well she can't convalesce here."

"Tea?" Kate broke into his thoughts.

"I'll make it. You sit."

The familiar kitchen. The old dresser on whose sharp corner he had cut his forehead and needed four stitches. His great-grandmother's dinner service, holding pride of place on high shelves. He sank into a pine chair and put his head in his trembling hands. He was still in shock, he knew that.

"Mack?"

"Not now, Kate."

Her cool fingers pulled at his hands and she moved close. He didn't need this. Her hold earlier that day had almost been his undoing. For a brief moment, seven years had slipped away and he'd fallen into the old illusion. But she was there again. The vanilla scent of her perfume, the soft warmth of her body. He let out a slow sigh as she held him, his own arms finding her, pressing her close. He relaxed in her hold, resting his head against her breasts. Just to feel her in his arms, move with the rise and fall of her chest, listen to the beat of her heart.

"Mack." Kate's soft voice drifted through his hazed senses. Her fingers gently stroked his short hair and he sighed against the caress. "She's going to be fine." He felt the impression of her lips in his hair.

It had been creeping up on him from the second he saw her at the Pennington Hoffer Ball. Seeing her weave through the guests, the subtle sway of her hips, the way her dress shimmered in soft pools of light. Ignoring the jolt of jealousy when male eyes followed her every movement. He had wanted to run before he made the idiotic mistake of talking to her. However, he'd found her hand on his arm and he began to lose his reason in the incredible blue of her eyes.

He still couldn't remember how they'd made it back to his hotel room.

It was stupid to feel this way. He closed his eyes. Insane to still love this woman.

The admission burned through him. But he would never admit it. Not a second time.

He wanted comfort. Nothing more, but her lips moved again, another light, gentle kiss on his forehead. And then another. She shouldn't. Mack lifted his head and dark eyes burned her. She really—

His mouth on hers, lips, tongues, teeth, hot and furious. Kate clung to him, aware with every second that it was wrong. Even as her hands dragged at his shirt, her fingers running fast over smooth skin.

No. She tore her lips away, her breathing hoarse, desperate. She tried to push him away. "This is wrong."

She watched as his breathing slowed. Mack's endless eyes sparked with a golden fire. And something else. "Yes," he said softly. He slid open kisses over her throat and Kate's resolve weakened. "It is. Very wrong."

She wanted to protest, knew that she should. But she was in Mack's arms again.

Mack stood and took her hand in his. Kate followed him too willingly out of the kitchen and up the narrow stairs. "My old room." He switched on a small lamp.

Kate stared around the smooth, cream walls, the soft rugs, the little array of ornaments on painted shelves. Her gaze skirted the big double bed. "Doesn't feel like a boy's room."

Mack smiled. "My mother jumped at the chance to redecorate when I left for University." The smiled faded and Kate felt his withdrawal.

"The doctor said she would make a full recovery."

"I know." He caressed her cheek, ran along her jaw, leaving a trail of burning skin. "I know."

Kate's heart thudded. It was almost painful. This was wrong. It would cause her heartache in the end. Yet, she couldn't deny herself more of Sean Mackenzie. She watched the slow, seductive smile spread over his handsome face, his dark eyes spark with lamp light. "It's so difficult to resist you." He focused on her lips.

"Then don't even try."

His gaze snapped up at the softly spoken words and Kate's mouth ran dry at the want she found there. Her tongue traced around her mouth to ease parched lips. She didn't imagine Mack's groan at her action. His lips were so close she could almost taste him, feel the warmth of his breath stir her skin.

The burn of his lips on hers. Slow. Soft. Tasting each other, wanting…

"Too many clothes, Kate." He lifted her cotton sweater over her head. His fingers made quick work of the zip on her skirt. Then lightly skimming her flesh, teasing her, making her arch into his touch, before he picked her up and laid her on his bed.

The duvet was cool under her bared skin as she sank into its thickness. Time slowed. Kate heard, felt the hoarse sound of her own breathing. Aching need tightened low in her pelvis and her fingers snatched at the heavy, cotton cover, crushing the material between taut hands.

All too slowly, Mack slid his white shirt over his stomach, his chest. The ripple of firm muscle under hair-roughened skin. Kate's mouth dried, her chest tightened, as lamp light spilled gold over his perfection. The dark peaks of his nipples that she ached to kiss, the impressive, well-defined abdominal muscles into which she wanted to sink her teeth…

The anticipation of touching him, of running fingers and a hot mouth over his silken skin, drove a fierce ache through her veins, making her all too aware of what was to come. And Mack knew. Knew that as he dropped his shirt to the floor, his slow fingers moving to his belt buckle. His dark gaze speared her and her breath caught. Such hunger. All for her.

"This is driving you crazy, isn't it, Kate?"

His voice, low, soft, stirred her skin. "Damn you, yes," she moaned.

He pulled at the top button of his black trousers, the zip dropping tooth by tooth. "Why rush?" he drawled. Mack had no idea why he was behaving like this. He wanted Kate, wanted to bury himself, lose himself inside her. No, he was lying. He knew why. He wanted this time, to extend the illusion that she loved him.

His trousers pooled at his feet.

The want was unbearable. Kate refused to look at the long, solid muscle of his thighs. Why was he doing this to her? Her need curled her fingers deeper into the duvet, until her knuckles showed white. It was hard to believe that she was with Mack as he taunted her with his slow aching delay.

She could easily get off the bed.

No. She couldn't.

Her body thrummed with the thought of the moment when his fingers first caressed her burning, tortured skin.

She fought to open her eyes, found him watching her with a gaze, which blazed hot trails over her almost nakedness. She licked parched lips and his jaw clenched. "Why are you doing this, Mack?"

His deep brown eyes narrowed on her. A slow finger ran, feather-light, over her flushed cheek. Kate couldn't deny the shiver that raced through her body, nor the faint moan that escaped her.

"I've never met a woman like you, Kate," Mack said softly. He knelt over her. His hand glided over her thigh and a smile grew as her moan deepened. "And this, you, are far too good."

"Yes," she sighed.

His fingertips trailed over her stomach, delayed on the swell of her breast, the hardened nub of her nipple through the thin fabric of her bra. Fire trailed in his slow, deliberate wake, the sensuous run of his short nails over her heated flesh jolting into her pelvis. How did he do this? He had barely touched her. Was this what loving him did to her? So close now. She slid her hands up the warm, smooth-muscled arms, fingers playing with the beautifully sharp definition, slipping over his neck to thread through his soft hair. Kate's gaze devoured his features, the sharp plane of jaw, his firm mouth, those eyes… "My God, you're beautiful." The heat of embarrassment shot through her as the words escaped.

A smile pulled at his lips. "Beautiful, Kate?"

Her bra, her panties were gone. His tongue teased over her nipple and she gasped, her unease forgotten. "Yes." Kate allowed herself to become lost in the moment, to lose herself in the man she loved.

"Beautiful," he said, before his mouth claimed hers again, a slow tongue flicking against hers.

His lips caressed her warm skin, gliding over her jaw, throat, clavicle. Kate couldn't help the little mewls of pleasure that escaped her. It was obvious Mack wanted to explore every inch of her body.

His tongue glided over her breast. Air cooled her skin in his wake and Kate closed her eyes, memorizing what his touch evoked. Her desire for him rioted again, washing away the unease of knowing that his heart belonged to someone else. Kate needed him. One more time, she told herself.

She gasped as his teeth grazed her nipple, growing waves of pleasure shooting down through her body. Kate arched against his mouth. Her mind fused and her guilt was forgotten. She was with Mack. And however much it hurt afterwards she had this time, this memory.

Warm, wet openmouthed kisses trailed over her skin to her other breast. Kate luxuriated in the feel of him caressing her body, stretching, into every kiss. More little moans of pleasure escaped her and Mack smiled in response. Kate's spine arched against the onslaught of his fingers, his mouth and tongue, the slide of his sweat-slicked body over hers. Her breaths came in short gasps. She wanted, needed, to feel Mack inside her. Her hips ground against him, hands firm on his buttocks, uncaring—

"You want me?" Mack's voice, rough, low, sent a shiver through her frame.

He was teasing her, brushing the edges of her heated flesh. Her need tightened her chest, ripped an ache through her that she wanted him to satisfy. "Mack. Please."

With one thrust, he buried himself deep within her.

"Oh God…"

Kate's eyes shot open and found Mack's. Held him. A gaze black with desire, gleaming, wanting her. The exquisite feel of skin against skin. Mack started to rock against her and Kate forgot everything else. She pulled his head down to her fierce mouth, losing herself in the dark taste of him.

She ripped her mouth away and buried her face into his neck, teeth nipping, biting, wanting him to know how he overwhelmed her, wanting him to feel the same. It used to be like this, giving herself totally to the man she loved. His moans were sweet to her senses, his breath sending shivers over her skin.

"Kate." The word was a pleasured sigh and his tongue traced the sensitive skin below her ear, lips reaching for her earlobe.

Someone cried out his name and Kate realized it was her. All control, all sense, evaporated as she splintered. Crushing, clinging, her arms, hands, fingers tight into his hot flesh, her hips, legs shifting, holding him deeper. One with him as their slick bodies raced through her orgasm. Mack followed her, groaning, collapsing, sighing into the damp skin of her neck.

She skimmed her fingers over his cheek, held his dark eyes. She gave him a slow, relaxed smile, pleasure still thrumming her nerves. Her lids slid shut and she sighed as Mack held her close. Within minutes, his breathing was even, slipping easily into sleep. Kate's last thoughts were melancholy before sleep claimed her too. Even as his name exploded from her lips, in that moment of release, Kate couldn't say the three extra words burning in her mind, aching on her tongue.

Mack loved someone else. He had said it again. He was only using her for sex.

Kate closed her eyes. Well, Beth had given her a way out. For her own sanity, she had to take it.

℣

Mack struggled out of sleep, sure that he had heard his mobile ringing. Still groggy, he pulled free from the woman in his arms and padded across the darkened room to where his jacket hung from a chair. He scratched at his untidy hair and pulled the mobile out of the inside pocket. "Mackenzie," he muttered, his voice hoarse.

"Mr. Mackenzie? It's the Royal. Your mother, Elisabeth Mackenzie, is awake and asking for you."

The fuzz shot from his brain. "I'll be right there."

He threw on his crumpled shirt. There had been no time the day before to think about fresh clothes, Angela could—

The duvet shifted. Mack remembered who was in his bed. He stared at the splay of black hair across the white cotton pillows, the soft blush to her warmed skin. Kate looked peaceful, beautiful.

Mack let out a slow sigh. She cared only for his money and herself, had cracked his heart wide open when he had discovered that fact. But he loved her. Despite that. After all, he had more money than he could spend in several lifetimes. But it was his family history almost repeating itself. "Kate?" He watched her eyes flutter open and a smile drift over her mouth.

"Mack."

At any other time, her tone would have him back in their bed, everything else forgotten. A wry smile pulled at his mouth. "I have to go to the hospital," he said, unable to deny himself a brief taste of her warm lips.

Kate arched and sighed, pulling at the weight of the duvet. She turned away. "Give my love to the budgerigar."

Mack left the room grinning. He'd forgotten how often he'd had a full conversation with Kate, only to discover that she was dreaming and didn't remember a thing. The car was there within ten minutes and Mack was soon on his way to the hospital. He relaxed back into the soft leather, closed his eyes and tried to ignore the chaos that churned through his life.

"Sir?"

Mack scrubbed at his bristled jaw, wishing he'd had the forethought to bring his shaving kit from his office. "What?"

"We're at the hospital."

He had fallen asleep. He glanced at his watch. Seven-twenty. "Thanks." Mack climbed out of the back seat. He made his way down the familiar corridors, the fear that had gripped him the day before almost gone. His mother was awake and wanted to see him. That had to be good, didn't it?

"Mack."

There were still too many machines hooked up to her body, and she looked pale, exhausted. Fierce bruising mottled her face. But there was that glimmer of life in Beth's eyes. Mack couldn't help the grin that broke over his face, the lift in his heart. "Will this stop your DIY now?"

Her smile grew but then she winced. "Don't make me laugh," she moaned. Her face slid into seriousness. "Mack, there's a reason I dragged you out at this godforsaken hour."

His gut tightened. "Have they changed the diagnosis?"

"No. Nothing like that." Her uninjured arm waved at the chair beside the bed. Reluctantly, Mack sat. "Yesterday is fuzzy. But I remember one thing." She grimaced. "I thought I was going to die."

"Mother—"

"No." Her hand squeezed his. "I should have told you this years ago." Her eyes closed and she sighed. "Edward married me for my money. The estate was in debt, more of the Colonel's mismanagement. I was young, stupid," her teeth bit at her lip, "and on the rebound." Her dark eyes fixed on the blanket and her voice was caught in past pain. "I thought he was playing with me. That I was a gauche girl, meant to amuse him."

"My father?" Mack was confused. It almost sounded as if she were talking about someone else.

"No." A wry smile. "Yes." Her eyes finally found his. "I cut all ties from him, from Robert and married Edward, his best friend. Spite, I suppose. I was a fool."

"Robert?" Mack's mind shot back to the Lodge's sunny front room, his mother's reticence over a certain photograph. "Robert Thorpe?"

"He went to work overseas but came back. I was already married, had been for six months. Robert thought I would be waiting for him. I thought he'd dumped me. Edward didn't care. He had access to my money. He said I could do what I liked. He wouldn't divorce me."

Mack stared. His mind refused to work. "What are you saying?"

"You're Robert Thorpe's son."

He was out of his chair. For years, he had thought that his mother had pined for his father, for Edward Mackenzie, that he had broken her heart. But now she was saying? "Are you sure?" The words were out and Mack's hands tightened into fists. He shouldn't ask his *mother* of all people—

"Yes." Her gaze dropped to where her fingers picked at the cellular blanket. "I never…with Edward." A smile twitched at her lips. "I couldn't."

Embarrassment constricted his gut and he found himself staring out at the little rockery, catching his own reflection in the thick glass. He suddenly wanted to see that photograph, to see if he could trace anything of himself in the stranger's features. "Did the Colonel know?"

"No," Beth said. "But your grandmother knew about Robert, whether she knew about you…I don't know. Greville Mackenzie married her for the estate. Nothing more. There was never any love lost there. Sometimes I wonder whether Edward was Greville's son."

"And Robert? What happened?"

"They were driving back to the estate. Edward had picked him up. Robert worked away a lot, family business. It was winter. They hit a patch of black ice. Edward, Robert and, I think her name was Karen, were killed instantly." Beth let out a breath, hissing against the pain.

"I don't remember him," Mack said. "I was seven, I should remember something."

"Robert worked abroad. And we were discrete. More discrete than Edward."

"But did he know? About me?"

"He loved you," she said, her eyes fierce on his. "Wanted to name you as his heir—but his family wouldn't let him." Her eyes closed briefly. "It caused years of in-fighting. Every Thorpe desperate for their branch to claim Robert's wealth." Her voice was almost to herself. "I had thought they'd sorted out an heir."

Mack sank into the chair beside the window and ran a shaking hand through his hair. "And I thought my life couldn't get any more insane."

"I had to tell you, Mack." The wry smile was back. "If only to offer the comfort that your child wouldn't be related to the Colonel."

"Yes," he murmured, distracted.

"You're staying at the Lodge? Then go back to bed, you look shattered."

"Am I like him?" he asked, looking up.

A sad smile pulled at her mouth and her eyes glimmered with tears. "More and more every day," she said softly. "He was brilliant, charismatic, funny. Devoted and loving. That's why I knew you couldn't marry again, well, not anyone other than Kate. You, like your father, can only give your heart once."

"And live with the consequences."

Beth's eyes narrowed. "Mack?"

"Kate married me for my money, both times. A business deal. She got support for her baby and I got—" He bit off the words. Beth didn't need to know the rest of the transaction.

"What?" There was that tone. The one she always used when he'd done something wrong and had yet to admit it. "You got?"

"It doesn't matter." He stood and straightened his rumpled jacket. "I should go."

"Has the Colonel got something to do with it?"

"Of course he hasn't."

"What did that old reprobate hold over you?"

"Mother."

"He was gloating at his dinner, only too pleased to rub my nose in your marriage, in the fact that Kate was pregnant." Her mouth thinned. "Has it got something to do with me?"

Mack cursed the fact that his mother was sometimes too clever. He should have kept his mouth shut, but her revelation had rattled him into blurting out some unwanted truths. He sighed. Damn it, he had to tell her. "He threatened to throw you out of the Lodge."

"He what?" Beth's anger obviously aggravated her ribs, her shoulder. She hissed and eased herself back into her pillow. She suddenly looked tired, old.

"See, I didn't want to tell you." Guilt rioted through him. "Are you all right?"

"Fine." She expelled a slow, pained breath. "The Lodge was given to me by your grandmother. He can't touch it."

"He found a loophole. He's within his rights."

"And that's why you married Kate?" There was a sadness to her voice.

"That, and she said the baby was mine." He couldn't say she'd sold him the child. Some things still hurt too much to be spoken aloud.

"You doubt it?"

"Yes." He shrugged. "No."

"It sounds like you need to sit down and have a proper talk with her, Mack. Don't think about the Colonel, about me. You've always loved her. Tell her."

"Yes, Mother." He didn't need this advice. He knew what he should do. It was just that he was…scared. Scared to expose himself again. It was a terrifying thought that he would love only her for all of his life… And that Kate didn't return his love. "I'll come back this afternoon. You should rest."

Her eyes were already closing, even as she tried to fight it. "Talk to her, Mack," she said, her voice growing soft with sleep. "I didn't tell Robert. And it caused us years of pain."

Mack placed a light kiss on her forehead and she sighed. "I'll see you later." He thought of Kate, probably still asleep in his bed. The fear clutched at him. He turned away from his mother's bed.

It seemed impossible.

Kate could, would, never love him.

Chapter Ten

Kate had thought about running. She had cash, enough to get her to the nearest town, and a card for an ATM machine. With money, she could get a train. Those thoughts had rushed through her brain as she lay in yet another cold bed. She had even gotten as far as writing Mack a letter detailing why she couldn't continue with the pretense.

But she knew that Mack would find her, as he had found her at Robert's. She needed to have it out with him, face to face. Sort it and move on. It was why she was sitting in Beth's kitchen garden with a cup of herbal tea. After she had expended some of her nervous energy on cleaning and clearing away the remains of Beth's breakfast, and other chores. Morning sunlight edged over the old wall and brought with it a welcome warmth, taking the chill from the air.

Why had she slept with him? Again. Why?

Kate closed her eyes and breathed in the calming scents of sage, lavender, the hint of lemon from her tea. She kept making the same mistakes. It was time to put away her self-destructive need for Mack. She could've coped. She could. Her own mother had provided for her and Francesca when their father had died when Francesca was only a few months old. But a stupid part of her had wanted to share the baby with Mack, hoping that it could mend their relationship.

"Stupid, stupid, stupid," she muttered. She swallowed the last of the cooling tea. Kate stared at her watch. Just gone nine. Mack must be at the hospital. Her gut twisted again as the unwanted thoughts leaked through. He could have asked her to go, left her a note, even called. She was being selfish. But a simple sign that he cared would've made everything real.

"What are you doing here?"

As if her day couldn't get any worse. "We stayed last night. Mack's at the hospital." Kate stood. The serenity of the little garden had just been blighted. "I'll tell him you called, Colonel."

Cold blue eyes narrowed on her. "You think you have your claws buried deep, don't you?"

Kate held back a sigh. All she had ever wanted was a peaceful life. "Colonel."

His bony hand grabbed her upper arm. Fingers tightened. Kate winced against his unexpected strength. "I have plans for my grandson. Ones which I will not allow you to jeopardize."

"Yes. Like trying to blackmail him into marriage!"

His fingers increased their grip and Kate yelped. "What do you know of that?"

The Colonel had to be losing it. He had said "no wife, no deal" in front of her. "You're hurting me." Her fingers tried to pry his away. She managed to struggle free, rubbing at bruised flesh. Her gaze darted back to the house, wondering if she should try to make a dash for the back door and lock it against the mad old man. "Look—"

"You're a sensible woman, Kate."

His tone of voice had her backing away. Why suddenly be nice to her after almost breaking her arm?

"Once Sean finds out, he'll cut you out without a penny." His voice was bitter. "I know my grandson." The false simper was back. "He wouldn't be as tolerant as me."

Tolerant? Colonel Mackenzie? Her mind fixed on his first words. "Finds out about what?"

Something flared in his cold eyes and the Colonel dug into his inside pocket and produced a long, white envelope. "I was going to show this to Sean, but if you leave, file for divorce, you may get something. He'll never forgive you, of course. However, if you make an attempt—"

"What are you rambling about?" Kate demanded.

His finger stabbed at her belly and Kate instinctively put her arms around her abdomen. "I have proof that he's not the father."

"You *are* insane." She stared at the letter. Had Anthea Charlton concocted lies to drive a wedge between herself and Mack? But that would hardly drive him into her arms. Angela? But Mack had said his PA was involved in a long-standing relationship. All color drained from her vision, the world suddenly cold and grey. That left only one person. "I'm not listening to his rubbish anymore."

Kate turned her back on the Colonel. It was all she could do to put one step in front of the other. Was there anything Francesca would not do?

"Don't you turn your back on me." The Colonel snatched at her arm, pulling her up. "Sean cannot claim a bastard as his own," he growled.

If the Colonel had waited only a few more hours, she would have followed his wishes. But she would never tell him that, give him that satisfaction. Kate now understood Mack's hatred for the vicious old man.

"What are you doing?"

Relief almost made her body sag, but Kate found the strength to pull her arm free. "Mack." She met his gaze and found only hard darkness. Nothing there for her.

"You need to read this." The Colonel strode past her and slapped the white envelope in Mack's hand.

Words froze in Kate's mouth. She could deny it, demand that Mack believe her, not her sister. But this was her opportunity. Wasn't it? Mack would turn away from her and she would be free. Kate bit at her lip. However, she would never confirm Francesca's nasty accusations. Definitely not in front of the Colonel.

"More letters."

Mack's tone made a shiver run over Kate's skin. More? Had Francesca already written to him? Had the ever-efficient Angela told him?

"She played you for a fool," the Colonel rasped. "Read that."

"I need to speak privately with my wife."

Mack stepped aside and dark eyes held her. Something burned in his relentless gaze. Fear gripped her. Belatedly, she wished she had followed her first instinct and fled the cottage.

Anger hardened the Colonel's withered face. "You can't let her get away with this. The baby isn't yours. I need—"

"What?" His eyes narrowed on the hated old man. "An heir? But you have me, Grandfather."

"I'm not discussing a private matter in front of her." The Colonel turned away and his cane began to stab at the path.

"Or is it *my* heir that you need?"

He watched the old man stop, his shoulders tighten. Mack began to curse. "You knew," he muttered. "All along, you knew."

The Colonel's spine straightened and he turned. A sour smile twisted his mouth. "Never cared for children. Not concerned with a wife. Land was what I wanted, so I married Isabel and got this place.

"Edward was the by-product of some affair." The glitter in his cold blue eyes made Mack's gut clench. "As were you." The Colonel's icy gaze slid to Kate and Mack saw her shudder. "Seems that your wife wanted to carry on the family tradition."

The blood drained from Kate's face at his words. Mack's hands tightened into fists. "Why is it important to you that Kate is carrying my child?"

The Colonel turned away again. "Tell your mother that she has a week's notice on the Lodge."

"A Thorpe heir? Succession? Is that what you wanted? Something you could offer someone in the family in return for what? The money I won't give you?"

He didn't stop. "She has a week. No longer."

"Mack—"

He didn't want her excuses. "Inside," he said.

Kate sank into an old pine chair and rested her elbows on the table. She hid her face in her hands. What that horrible man had said. Denying Mack his father, yet he seemed to know. A Thorpe heir? Beth and Robert Thorpe? Thoughts whirled through her head and she tried to find something to ground her. She closed her eyes. It didn't help.

And Francesca.

Kate didn't know what to do. She was the intruder, bursting into a five-year relationship. Obligation and necessity had forced Mack to marry her. Now Francesca had removed all obstacles for him. Kate wiped at the tear forming under her eyelid, slipping onto her lashes. She loved him. But she couldn't stay. He loved her sister.

Footsteps over the old tiles. She didn't look up.

"Interesting read."

The letter slapped on to the table.

"Recognize the handwriting?" The slide of paper over the clean, wooden surface. "Look at it, Kate."

Reluctantly, she opened her eyes and stared at the letter. Two letters. Francesca's large, flowing script. And then the other. Small, neat. Her fingers lightly touched the words. It looked like… "I didn't write this," she said, words coming out of her mouth before she could think. Had her sister added forgery to her list of talents?

"No?"

The disbelief in his voice stabbed at her. Emotion churned through Kate, making her head light, her eyes ache with tears. Saying nothing, that was her plan. She couldn't confirm Francesca's lies, but to deny them… Kate couldn't throw away her chance to make a break from Mack, no matter how painful. She let out a slow sigh and straightened her shoulders. "Believe what you like, Mack," she said. Her gaze met his and she hoped the shine of unshed tears had left her. "How's Beth?"

"Believe what I like?" he grated. He jerked away from the table, his hand tight over his mouth. Kate saw the muscles in his jaw working out his anger. He turned back, his eyes burning into hers. "You state that you've been 'involved' with the father for three years."

Kate climbed on to her feet and tried to ignore the ache in her gut. Even her ribs hurt. Mack had always believed Francesca over her. Didn't that show how he loved her? She shrugged. "My sister seems to like to keep you informed of my life." She ran a hand through her loose hair, hissing as the action stretched her ribs. She had obviously overdone the cleaning that morning. "I'm hungry. Would you like breakfast?"

He grabbed at her arms. "Damn it Kate, deny this."

Mack's fingers pressed into already bruised flesh and Kate yelped. "You're hurting me."

He instantly released her, his hands scrubbing over his face, running through his hair. "Is it Thorpe?"

"Why does it matter, Mack?" she said, rubbing at her arms. She leaned against the deep ceramic sink. "You married me for this place." She flicked her fingers around the shadowy kitchen. "Would have done that without me being pregnant." Briefly, she wondered how Francesca had felt about that. She couldn't see her sister "banging out some decent heirs", as the Colonel had so elegantly phrased it. Kate couldn't imagine Francesca letting anything interfere with her perfect figure. She gripped the sink and the nausea rose again. Would Mack have made it part of their deal? "But that's all fallen away now. I see no reason why we should stay married. Do you?"

Kate couldn't look at him when she asked the question. It was over. It had to be less painful breaking away from him now. To see him turning away from a baby whose paternity he had always doubted. No. She couldn't bear it.

"There's nothing that could keep us together, Kate," he said, his voice calm, quiet. "I should never have entered into this charade."

All hope died in her. Some insane part of her had wanted him to declare that he loved her. "Yes." But this had to be better, didn't it? He had found happiness with Francesca. Not her. And she did want Mack to be happy. She straightened and her fingers released their bloodless hold on the sink. She had to change the subject. "How was Beth this morning?"

"Fine, fine," he said. "Tired."

Kate splashed water into the kettle and plugged it in. She had just dissolved her marriage, but time still moved on, her body still demanded to be fed. She moved to the fridge, her legs heavy, and stared sightless at the contents.

"What do you want?"

She started at the hand on her shoulder. What did she want?

"Something cooked?"

Food, he was asking about food. "I can make it myself, Mack."

"Is that why you've had the door open so long, everything's starting to melt?"

Kate found herself being pushed back into a chair and watching as Mack made her breakfast. Why did he have to be nice now? Couldn't he ignore her? Go and have a five-hour conversation with Francesca?

"Eat."

She blinked. Time had flown and she had just sat there, staring, obviously in shock. Like an automaton, she picked up the knife and fork and began to eat.

"Will Thorpe not support your lifestyle?"

Kate swallowed and realized that she had eaten a slice of sausage. She looked down at the plate. She'd demolished the cooked breakfast without tasting any of it. She didn't even like fried bread. "Robert's got nothing to do with this, Mack."

"But you'd like a slice of my money as a parting present, wouldn't you, Kate?"

Color slashed across her cheeks. It had crossed her mind earlier as she sat at Beth's little writing desk, trying to compose her leaving letter. It pained her to still need his money. "A loan," she murmured. "I remortgaged three years ago." And stupidly gave the money to her sister.

"Frittered it away and lost your flat." Mack pinched at the bridge of his nose with his thumb and forefinger. "You'll have a baby to care for, Kate. This can't continue. You know that."

She didn't need his lecture. He should be talking to his profligate mistress. "Thank you for the breakfast," she said, rising to her feet. "I need to sleep."

"Kate—"

Anger flared at his patronizing tone. "My life is not your concern, Mack. I've asked you for a loan. You can say yes or no. And now that I won't have your mistress like a dead weight around my neck—" She bit off the rest of her words and blew out bad air. "Wake me when you next want to visit Beth. I'd like to say goodbye."

"My mistress?"

"I'm going to bed."

"You keep throwing these women at me."

Kate turned, stared at him. "*I* keep throwing these women? Wherever I turn there's some woman claiming you."

"Are you jealous, Kate?"

Fury rattled through her. "You and Francesca deserve each other."

Mack sighed. "Now it's Francesca?"

"Oh please." Kate looked up at him, anger making her back straight. "Why deny it? You've been together five years. How did she take her demotion? Or was she not willing to produce babies on demand?"

"This is ridiculous." Mack began to clear the plates into the dishwasher. "Not that it's any of your business, but Francesca and I don't have that kind of relationship."

"No, she just bleeds you for money."

Mack's eyes narrowed and Kate saw the flare of anger in his hardened face. "Following your example?"

"I never wanted a penny from you." Kate turned before her fury blurted out words Mack shouldn't hear.

"Pennies were never enough," Mack grated. "That settlement, your jewelry, your rings—"

"Here." She yanked her wedding and engagement rings from her finger and slapped them against the table, feeling the diamond dig hard into her palm. "Find someone to make better use of them."

"Freely given this time?"

Kate walked away.

"What, no little ticket? Paying through the nose for something I bought in the first place?"

"Now who's not making sense?"

Mack caught her at the foot of the stairs, twisting her to face him. "You didn't think I'd find out that you'd pawned your wedding rings?"

Kate stared at him. "What are you talking about?" She shrugged her shoulder out of his grip. "They were worth money. So you, being so very conscious of that, took them back."

Mack laughed, a hard, bitter sound. "And I suppose you never cashed the check, either?"

"Mack, I'm tired." She grabbed at the banister rail and hauled herself up the narrow stairs. A headache pulsed at the edges of her skull and it made thinking painful. She wanted to sleep. "And you know that I never took a penny of the settlement." The old ache rose again and her voice was a whisper. "You called me a whore. How could I?"

Mack watched Kate climb the stairs. He wanted to follow her, wrap her in his arms, say that— He sighed. The letter his grandfather had given him hurt. To know, to have evidence that the child she carried wasn't his. He closed his eyes. But he could put that aside. He would've loved the baby, did love the baby, because it was a part of Kate.

He fumbled in his trouser pocket and pulled out the folded note he had found on his mother's writing desk. He already knew the words by heart, but he scanned them again. Short, and to the point. And the phrase that stabbed at him, "…our marriage is a pretense. Love is obviously fixed elsewhere."

Kate had called an end to the marriage. She didn't love him, she loved someone else. He should be relieved that he hadn't exposed his already battered heart yet again. He should. But he wanted to hold her, kiss away the strain growing lines around her eyes. "I'm an idiot," he muttered, turning back to the kitchen.

Francesca's letter waited for him on the table. And Kate's trying to deny that she hadn't pawned her rings, spent every penny of her divorce settlement was ridiculous. Did she take him for a total fool? Mack sank into the chair and a wry smile tugged at is mouth. "I *am* a total fool."

Evidence that she had married him for his money had driven him into a rage and he'd divorced Kate without a second thought. Found a false solace in Angela. But there had never been anyone who could replace her. The years alone had taught him that. Guilt stirred in his gut. Had he kept in touch with Francesca as a link to her sister?

Yes, he was a fool. He stared at the letter, the hint of lavender from Francesca's scented paper too strong. "I'm certifiable." Mack let out a slow breath. "Even with that, I still love her."

„⁍

Kate rubbed at the niggling ache in her side. Mack marched ahead as usual and she found herself breathless in his wake. Had the hospital corridor been this long before?

Sleep had eluded her. Her mind had spun with the nightmare her life had turned into, her head throbbing. And she had found it impossible to find a comfortable position to lie. Her side ached, spikes of pain shooting over her ribs as she twisted over the mattress. Cleaning was definitely not good for her.

"Are you all right?"

The question surprised her, as did the fingers gently lifting her jaw. She saw the shine of concern in Mack's dark eyes and it pierced her heart. He had to stop doing that. Kate didn't need the pretense of caring. "Fine." She stepped back from his light touch. "We should go in."

"Yes."

Mack let her precede him into the small hospital room. The sharp, antiseptic odor concentrated in the confirmed space and her stomach spasmed. "How are you feeling, Beth?" she asked, fixing a smile on her mouth.

"More awake." Her dark gaze shifted over her head to look at Mack and briefly Beth closed her eyes. "But I still feel like the house actually fell on me."

"So you're a wicked witch now?"

"Thanks, Mack, that makes me feel so much better."

Kate slid into one of the chairs placed beside Beth's bed and wished that she could join Mack as he traded witticisms with his mother. Absently, she rubbed at her side. The sharp smells made her breath catch. "Sorry," she murmured. "I've still got my over keen pregnancy nose." She flitted a smile and moved towards the door. "I need some air."

She was out of the room before Mack could offer more of his false concern. Kate headed for a small quadrangle of greenery she had spotted on her way in. It hurt and it helped to be away from Mack. She pushed at the heavy doors, noticing that a few mobile patients and hospital staff had also gravitated to the little garden.

"Kate?"

Inwardly, she cursed. She had wanted quiet time, time to sit, stare at flowers and not think. "James. Hello." She sat on the bench beside Mack's friend. "We've just arrived. The hospital smell got to me and I needed to escape."

James grinned. "I'm grabbing a ten minute break." His eyes narrowed. "Are you having trouble breathing?"

Kate gave him a rueful smile. "A bit. My ribs hurt." She stared as he took her wrist, measuring her pulse.

"Way too fast," he muttered. "Kate, would you mind coming to my office? I need to listen to your chest."

She blinked. "All right," she said.

ℰℐ

The knock on the door made Mack look up from his paper. He glanced back to his mother, quietly sleeping. Finally, Kate had— He forced a smile as James Roby stuck his head into the room. "James." A cold dread ran over his skin. "Is everything okay?"

"Can I have a private word?"

Mack's heart contracted. "What is it?"

James gaze flicked to the sleeping woman. "Come to my office."

Like an automaton, Mack rose to his feet and followed his old friend out of the room and into the busy corridor. They followed a maze of twists and turns, until James stopped at a door. Mack moved forward and found Kate sitting in a chair, her face white and what looked like fear in her eyes.

"Have a seat." James pointed to a chair beside Kate.

Mack fell into it, his anxiety increasing when a small hand slid into his and gripped it. Hard.

"I've examined Kate." James sat behind his cluttered desk. "She's having trouble breathing, has developed a sudden sharp pain over her ribs and her pulse—"

"What's wrong?" Mack demanded.

His friend sat back into his deep chair. "I listened to her chest. There's a quietness at the base of her right lung. It could be that one lung is shorter than the other. But it could also mean that her lung has partially collapsed. Or there is the possibility of a clot." The doctor let out a slow breath. "A clot is potentially fatal."

Mack stared. He tore his eyes away from James to stare at Kate. Terror washed over him. "But she's pregnant," he whispered. Not Kate. Not his baby. "What can you do?"

"We need to do tests," James said. "X-ray, gamma camera. Kate's already agreed to an injection of fragmin, a blood thinner, as a precaution."

"But the baby," Mack said.

"There is very small risk to the fetus, but the injection of radioactive material will be reduced because Kate's pregnant." James sat forward, his face grave. "No matter how slight the risk, we have to rule out a clot, Mack. It is that worrying."

The words tightened his gut. And Mack's world crashed around him.

Chapter Eleven

Kate tried to make herself comfortable on the gurney surrounded by grey curtains. James had admitted her to Medical Assessment and now she was waiting for the battery of tests to begin. It couldn't be happening. Her ribs were sore, that was all. Nothing major. Nothing life threatening.

She clutched at the thin sheet and her eyes closed against the sudden riot of fear.

"Kate?"

Mack's hand, prying her fingers from the crumpled sheet, holding them, his thumb slowly circling her palm. "You'll both be fine."

"It's the last time I clean up for your mother," she said and caught his twitch of a smile.

"She's leaving the estate," he said, his attention fixed on her hand. "I'd offered her the cottage before, the one built behind my house. This time she's accepted."

"Beth had no choice."

"No."

Kate shifted uneasily, wincing against the sudden spurt of pain across her chest. "About what your grandfather said…"

Mack released her hand and ran his fingers through his untidy hair. "It's true." A bleak smile inched across his mouth. "And it's some small relief that I'm absolutely no relation to the old monster."

"For me too," Kate said.

He had worried about the baby, even when he thought it was another man's child. She didn't think it possible, but she loved the man more. "This is your baby, Mack." Her gaze dropped to the sheet, scared that he would begin to argue again. "That letter...I never..." Despite all that Francesca had done, Kate couldn't tell Mack the truth about the woman he loved. She shrugged and winced.

"Kate, it—"

"Good afternoon." The curtains surrounding her bed shot back and a nurse wheeled a trolley into the cramped space. The woman smiled and began to sort through an assortment of wires and pads. "This is the ECG. I just need to stick wires on you."

The nurse babbled on, placing pads on Kate's leg, arm, chest. Kate stared at the tiled ceiling and tried to ease her pained breathing. She wondered what Mack had been going to say.

"Done," the nurse declared, pulling at the sticky pads. She smiled. "The blood trolley's on its way round."

"I hate needles."

"I know," Mack said. "Don't look."

All too quickly, someone was tapping her veins and there was an uncomfortable fizzing as the nurse drew blood. Kate winced. She felt only the bone-breaking grip on Mack's hand, gained comfort and strength from his steady hold. It was insane. Only hours before they had agreed to divorce. Yet here he was. Kate wanted to believe that it was something more than a twisted sense of obligation, but she knew she was holding onto a false hope. In a way, she would prefer him to leave. He brought with him the constant reminder that he would never be hers.

Her head felt light and she relaxed back on to the bed. She listened to her own breathing.

"Are you all right?"

Mack's soft voice seemed distant. Kate twitched a smile. "Needles and blood," she said. "Not a good combination for me." She pulled her hand free from his and ran fingers through her hair, her palm wiping at the beads of sweat on her forehead. "You don't have to stay, Mack." She stared at the pitted surface of the tiles high above her head. "Your mother will be worried. Wonder where you've gone."

"Kate."

"I'll be fine." She made a smile work across wax lips. Kate met his dark gaze and watched it narrow. "You should be with her. You shouldn't feel obliged to sit with me."

"Obliged? That's—"

"There you are!"

Not her. Not now.

"I stopped by your office. Angela said that Beth was ill." Kate heard the smile in her voice. "I didn't think. I just dropped everything and came. Angela also insisted I bring your essentials." Her fingers rasped over the stubble on Mack's jaw. Kate's heart gave a painful thud at such an intimate gesture. "Seems she was right."

"So." Francesca scraped a chair over smooth, vinyl tiles. "Is this part of the normal routine?"

She met her sister's candid, smiling gaze. How could she act as if she had never written that letter, all of those lies? Kate swallowed back against the sour taste of bitterness. "No," she said. "They're simply checking a few things out."

Concern shone in Francesca's pale blue eyes. "Everything's all right, isn't it?"

"Fine." Kate would not expose her fear. Francesca had hurt her too much already. The time for sharing with her sister had long passed.

"Kate—" Mack began.

Now he had something to keep from his mistress. "Mack?"

Kate watched his fingers drag through disheveled hair. He looked tired, worn. And she hated the fact that she wanted to hold him, tell him not to worry, that everything would be all right. But she saw how close Francesca was. The way her forearm rested against the back of his chair. How her body leaned...

Mack wasn't hers. Kate held back a sigh.

"So how's Beth?" Francesca asked. Concern edged her voice. "Angela gave me only sketchy details."

"She's fine."

A smile curved Francesca's lips. "That symptom seems to be catching."

His mouth twitched and Kate knew he was trying not to laugh in return. She was making the right decision. Mack obviously had a great deal of affection—*be honest, Kate*—of love, for Francesca. Her sister made him smile, even in the worst of times. Kate's throat ached with unshed tears. She couldn't compete.

The swift slide of the curtain made her start. "Kate Hartley?" A porter flipped at the paper attached to the clipboard at the end of her gurney.

Kate swallowed. "That's me."

The man smiled. "Time for your X-ray."

The porter wheeled Kate beyond the grey double doors. They slapped back into place and Mack closed his eyes. This wasn't happening. This wasn't—

"Mack?"

Francesca's slender hand slid into his. Her rich, jasmine scent cut through the antiseptic odor pervading the waiting area.

"I've done something stupid."

"Not now, Francesca."

"But you don't understand," she said. The wheedling tone sharpened the edge of a rising headache. "He threatened me."

"My grandfather?"

Mack took his gaze, briefly, from the closed doors. His question had met with a stunned silence. A wry smile pulled at his mouth. He had never seen Francesca lost for words before. Even her face had lost color; eyes pale and huge.

"Y-yes. He threatened horrible things. I didn't know what to do. I wanted to tell you before…before you married." Her gaze dropped to her lap and she let out a slow breath. "I should have. But Kate can be vindictive. I was scared."

Mack's attention was back on the door. Something beyond. A porter. His heart squeezed, thickened thuds making his chest ache. A wheelchair. A teenage boy. Not Kate. Mack sighed. Some of Francesca's words penetrated. "Kate? Vindictive?"

A sheen of tears brightened her eyes. "She's always been, jealous, I suppose." She shrugged and looked away.

"Of what?"

Her head snapped back. Mack blinked. The shine to her eyes, the trace of wetness was gone. A glimmer instead, of what, anger? That vanished and the sad, almost doleful look was back. And for the first time since he'd known her, Mack felt a certain deliberate falseness in Francesca.

"Of how I look, of how I act." She tutted. "Poor Kate."

Mack stared at her. Kate was beautiful, forthright, intelligent. But he did remember their first date and Kate's lack of confidence in her own beauty. He thought he'd shown her just how beautiful she was.

Mack looked at the hand that held his, at the glossily false, French polished nails. He wanted Kate's hand there. Slender fingers with neatly trimmed, clean nails. Sensible, but so much more elegant. However, Kate had made her choice. Her love was fixed elsewhere. In that minute, an angered need gripped him. "Who is he?"

"Who?"

"You said a 'work colleague'."

Francesca paused. She fixed her gaze on the X-ray Department doors. "You've seen the letters?"

"Yes." Mack's eyes narrowed. "Is it Robert Thorpe?"

"Robert?" Francesca snatched her hand away, straightened in the plastic seat. Her finger swept back loose, black hair. "I hardly think that Robert has *any* interest in Kate."

Mack blinked.

"Oh, they're acquaintances," she continued. "Work in the same department, but he would never—"

"You're protecting her now."

"What?" A flush had risen on Francesca's flawless cheeks. "What do you mean?"

"I've seen them together." The next words were said through gritted teeth. "*Found* them together."

"Robert?"

Mack gave her a bitter smile. "So your notoriously fickle heart has finally been touched."

Francesca glared at him. "Don't be ridiculous. And I don't think that's at all funny."

He scratched his fingers through his hair, welcoming the pain of his nails against his scalp. "No, it's not."

"She would have told me." Francesca almost sounded as if she was in shock. "Kate tells me everything. Always has. She would've said Robert, not—"

The bang of the doors broke into her run of words. He forgot his conversation with Francesca. Kate looked pale, dark shadows mottling the skin under her eyes. But she still smiled up at him. Mack's heart clenched.

"Everything go okay?"

The words sounded trite. But they were the only ones he could force out of his mouth. He took over the pushing of her wheelchair, dimly aware that Francesca tagged along behind him.

"They wrapped me in lead," she said.

"I bet that looked attractive."

"Remind me not to include it in my winter wardrobe."

"Too heavy?"

"Wrong color."

He wanted to kiss her. Hold her. Protect her.

"They said they'd pass the results to Dr. Roby, James."

Her voice trembled and it tore a fresh wound in his heart. "You'll both be fine."

Kate looked up at him.

And he knew then how artificial Francesca was. Kate had been crying. Not the pretense her sister had shown. The rims of her eyes were red, her long eyelashes spiky with tears. Worry gnawed at her. He saw it in the way her hands balled into bloodless fists, the tight press of her lips. "I promise. It'll be James being overcautious."

Her eyes closed. For a brief instant, before she turned away, Mack held the impression of her eyelids—delicate veins visible through translucent skin. A fragility that he didn't want to acknowledge. Kate was fire and passion. She had an inner strength.

"I may not have to go to Nuclear Medicine, if this X-ray looks clear." He heard the fight in her voice; the tremor suppressed.

Mack smiled, proud that she could be positive. "Missing out on your chance to glow in the dark?"

"Mr. Funny," she muttered, but the strain had eased from her voice. She looked up and her smile was sharp, wicked. "You missed your vocation, Mack. The entertainment world lost a very *mediocre* comedian."

His mother was right.

He would never love another woman. Kate had his heart, bitter and worn as it was. He met her smile. Robert Thorpe, his cousin, was a very lucky man.

෬

The icy rush of saline coursed along her vein. Kate winced and fixed her attention on the mass of complicated, steel grey equipment off to her left.

"That's clear." The radiographer injected another clear liquid into the vent on Kate's wrist. "If you look at the screen, you can see this spread through your lungs."

Kate closed her eyes. The X-ray had ruled out a partially collapsed lung. But James wanted to make absolutely certain that there was no risk of a clot. So now she was sitting in a metal chair, waiting to be bombarded with gamma radiation.

She concentrated on slow breaths. Breathing in. Breathing out. That brought a tight pain across her ribs. She was scared. Scared for her baby, for herself. And Mack.

The image of them together. Francesca sitting too close, so close that their shoulders touched. The brief flash of Mack's smile, her sister glaring at him. Had they been arguing? Francesca wondering why *she* was there, after making it very obvious how involved she was in Mack's life.

Loving him was hopeless. Stupid. But she couldn't stop. Kate sighed.

"Try to sit perfectly still."

Kate straightened. The radiographer turned her body. "Sorry."

"Just two more, then we're done."

She didn't want to dwell on how considerate Mack was being, how his humor had lessened the wash of fear. He had squeezed her hand as James said they should eliminate all risk. Appeared as if he might wrap strong arms around her, hold her when the radiographer came to the waiting room to collect her.

Francesca had stopped that. Sharp-nailed fingers gently caressed the back of his hand. That voice. Soft. Over intimate. "Mack. You know how small my car is. Angela packed it to bursting. Kate will be ages, won't you?"

Kate forced a smile to work its way over her lips. She remembered telling herself that she had no right to love him. His pity hurt. "I imagine so." She saw the gleam in her sister's eyes. Something almost bitter. "I'm sure James can show you somewhere to shave and change."

"Kate—"

"I've already said that I don't need your sympathy."

His familiar shuttered look slid down over his face. "If that's how you want it."

"Yes." She followed the radiographer out of the sunny room into the labyrinth of corridors. The door banged shut a second time and Kate knew that Mack and Francesca had left. Stupidly, her heart ached.

"All done."

Kate blinked and struggled down from the metal chair. She swallowed and rubbed damp palms together. She wanted to ask whether the woman had seen anything. But the words wouldn't come. Instead, she asked, "What happens now?"

"I'll examine the data and write a report for Dr. Roby." The radiographer smiled. "But my initial impression is that it's fine."

Kate felt light, almost giddy. A weight lifted after hours of worry. "Really?" Her heart was pounding and she couldn't control the tremor to her hands. "I'm fine? There's nothing?"

"It looks good." The woman opened the door to the room, waving Kate out before her. "Head back to the waiting room. You've people waiting, haven't you?"

Color rose under her cheeks. "They couldn't stay."

The radiographer gave a too-bright smile, her fingers gently squeezing her shoulder. Someone else feeling sorry for her. "Then a porter will take you back to Medical Assessment."

She was well. Kate had to keep reminding herself of the fact. However, the euphoria had slipped all too quickly. She was back where she had started. With everything. "At least I won't see the look of pity in his eyes anymore. Francesca has his love. Not me." And she had thought that the previous night would have made a difference. But that had only been sex. Again. A desperate grasping of life against the fear of death. Nothing more.

"Kate. I'll take you back."

She sank into the wheelchair. Not her sister. Not now. "I can wait for the porter."

"Don't be silly."

With her pleasant voice for the benefit of the staff and patients in the waiting room, Kate could hardly refuse. "I'm tired, Francesca."

The door slid back into place and they were out in the semi-silence of the corridor. "You've always had everything, haven't you, Kate?"

She was stung. "*I've* always had everything? You've stripped from me every penny I ever had." Kate ran a shaking hand over her face. That accusation had been the last thing she expected from her sister. "Look, I'm not feeling my best—"

"I refuse to pander to you."

"Nice of you to show your concern." Kate wondered if Francesca even knew what her series of tests had planned to determine. Probably not. And it appeared as if she didn't care.

"There's nothing wrong with you, Kate. There never was," Francesca continued, her voice bitter. She jerked the wheelchair forward and set a fast pace. The clack, clack, clack of her expensive shoes cut the short silence. "This is all to get Mack feeling sorrier for you than he already does."

The words cut and fresh tears burned. "What did I do wrong, Francesca? After Mum died, I did everything I could—"

"Oh please," Francesca grated. "I've always had to crawl and beg for anything from you. At least Mack never judges. He gives me what I ask for freely."

"Freely." Kate pushed her mind away from uncharitable thoughts, on exactly how Francesca paid for Mack's gifts.

"Or he did. I'm assuming there's been a mistake with this month's allowance."

Kate blinked. Mack had stopped bankrolling Francesca? It didn't seem possible.

"It'll be an oversight." Her sister sighed and there was a run of oversweet compassion to her voice. "The last few weeks have been trying for him. He told me he never wanted you back in his life."

Francesca knew where to hurt. The sprig of hope in Kate withered. She had to stop imagining there was any kind of future for her and Mack. "I know."

"And as for Robert."

"Robert?"

"You're supposed to be his 'friend'."

Kate was confused. "I am."

Francesca's laugh was hard, bitter. "Yes, as you're a good sister."

And she was in no mood for more of her games. "Fran, what are you talking about?"

"Mack knows what you are. But Robert? I thought you might have some consideration for how I—" Francesca bit down on the rest of the sentence. There was a strain to her voice when further words came. "Mack knows he's the father."

"You told him *that?*" Kate twisted her neck to stare up at her sister. "And your horrible letter. 'Work colleague'? So now you've filled in the blank."

Francesca's eyes were cold. "Mack told *me.*"

The pieces finally began to slot into place. And it revealed to Kate the depth of her sister's greed; what she would do. "You're jealous. You've been with Mack for five years, profess to love him. But it's his money that keeps you. Nothing more." The irony wasn't lost on Kate. He had abandoned her for that very reason. Her heart tightened. There was obviously more love there than he had ever had for her. Mack wasn't a stupid man. Far from it. He had to be ignoring the fact that Francesca didn't love him. Kate briefly closed her eyes. He deserved better. "You love Robert. But he's poor—"

"That's ridiculous," Francesca said, but color burned across her flawless cheeks. "You're the one chasing after two men. One of whom proposed marriage to me, only days before you turned up pregnant by another man."

"What?"

Kate's heart stopped. She had to believe it was a lie, one said to belittle. Mack had said he could think of no one else for the charade. Had he offered the real thing to Francesca?

"Upset that he's toying with you? Mack loves me." She laughed. "You didn't think he was falling for you, did you?" Her smile was sharp. "You did. Have I spoilt your thrill of twisting two men around your finger?"

Kate looked down at her knotted hands. Tears spilled cold onto her cheeks. But Francesca hadn't finished and gave a final twist.

"Mack's mine. Heart and soul." The quiet venom to her voice stabbed at Kate. "And Robert will be too."

"You're not playing your games with him." Mack loved Francesca. Kate would do everything in her power to stop her from breaking his heart. No matter what the cost. "You've made your life with Mack." She glared at her sister. "He's asked you to marry him."

"I'm simply following your example, sister dear."

"No."

All of their lives were a mess. Guilt tore at her. Guilt for pushing Mack into this decision to marry her. Guilt for sleeping with him, when she knew he was in love with someone else.

"Mack and I are divorcing."

Francesca stopped beside Kate's assigned cubicle. "So you've made your decision." She swept a tendril of fiercely black hair from her eyes. Her lips were thin, skin drawn. "I won't forgive you for this."

Kate pushed herself out of the wheelchair, hissing as she jarred sore ribs. She was tired and hungry and miserable. Words she never meant to speak came out. "You can't forgive me? You destroyed my first marriage in a fit of pique. And now you're going to destroy the man I…" Kate shook her head. She would not admit that she loved Mack. She didn't want to witness that little triumph on Francesca's face. "What's the use?" She sighed and climbed on to the thin comfort of the gurney. She lay down, trying to find a restful position. "Just go away, Francesca."

Kate gave her scowling sister a resigned smile. "You've nothing with which to threaten me. Not anymore. Every threat's used up."

Francesca's returning smile was sharp and unease crept through Kate. But what was left to spin? "Not every threat," she said. "Goodbye Kate. I doubt we'll speak again."

Chapter Twelve

It was pity.

And now that the threat to her life had proven false, all concern had dried up. Kate sank back into the soft leather, adjusting the seat belt as it snagged across her ribs. Why did she expect anything else? Kate held back a sigh. At least she had the consolation that Francesca wouldn't be staying at the Lodge.

The car crunched over the gravel drive and pulled to a slow stop. "Are...are you staying here tonight?" Kate hoped her words didn't sound desperate. And she knew she wasn't being fair. Mack would want to find comfort in Francesca. As weak as that was.

Mack climbed out of the car. He didn't reply.

"That's a yes then."

He was already at the door, a heavy holdall at his feet. Kate watched the long, sleek car skid out of the short drive and roar off into the fading light. There was silence. Lavender grew in large pots by the door and Kate brushed her fingers over the delicate flowers. She breathed in the soft scent, hoping to find a scrap of calm in their fragrance. Her heart slowed and her mind cleared. Yes. She knew what she had to do.

"I'll arrange to leave in the morning."

"You do that," Mack muttered, the key finally turning in the old lock. The door swung open and he disappeared into the narrow hallway.

Kate let out a slow breath. "Definitely gotten over the pity stage."

The door closed behind her with a quiet click. For a brief moment, she wondered if Francesca had woven some new lie, but that hardly seemed possible. There was nothing left that could sour Mack towards her any further. No. He had just shifted back into his usual dislike after a short period of weakness.

Kate's stomach rumbled and she rubbed an absent hand over it. Occupy her time with cooking. That was a plan.

"Would you like something to eat, Mack?"

"No."

"Fine." Kate rummaged through cupboards and the fridge. Fresh pasta. Tuna. Various vegetables and herbs to make a sauce. Kate deliberately made too much. Mack had to be hungry.

She was alone in the kitchen as she prepared her meal. The telephone rang briefly. Kate looked up from taking her concoction from under the grill. She heard Mack's deep tones and then the slam of the front room door.

Kate sighed and set the hot dish on the wooden counter. She rubbed at her side. The pain was easing, almost gone. Time and painkillers doing their job. The sizzling smells of onions, mushrooms, cheese made her stomach groan. Her appetite was returning. Finally, to be over the morning sickness. She put her husband from her mind and got on with the job of eating.

"What the hell is going on, Kate?"

The final forkful was halfway to her mouth. Her gaze shot to the man blocking the doorway. The food was suddenly heavy in her stomach and she dropped the fork back to the plate with a clatter. "What now, Mack?"

His angry gaze slashed over her but Kate was too tired. She had planned to sleep after she had eaten, her head was fuzzy and her aching body cried out for rest. However, Mack seemed to want to fight.

"That was Thorpe."

"Robert?"

"Why did you give him this number?"

Kate sighed. "How could I do that? I don't even know what it is. Look," she pushed herself up onto weary legs, "can we have this particular fight in the morning? You've had a horrible day. *I've* had a horrible day. I'd like to sleep."

Anger sizzled off Mack, his jaw hard, eyes alight with that fire. She had to remember she couldn't find him attractive. Yet his intoxicating, subtle scent wove around her, through her. Made her pulse quicken. It was stress. That's all. She didn't want him. She didn't. Crawling in a soft bed, worming herself under a heavy duvet, letting sleep take her. That's what she needed. Not—

His warm, strong hand closed over her jaw, fingertips caught in her hair. His voice grated. "What are you playing at now?"

"I don't play games."

"Of course you don't."

His hand pulled away and cool air washed the warmth from her skin. Kate pushed down the sudden ache. "Excuse me," she said, her voice subdued. Mack moved, but she still had to slide past him. The rub of his thighs against her own, the heat of his skin through his shirt. Damn it, she had to escape, escape before she stopped and let her hands explore—

"Don't you want to know what he had to say for himself?"

Kate let out a slow sigh. So close to getting away. "What?"

"That you're not to go ahead with the abortion."

Her heart contracted, felt like a stone in her chest. Slow muscles lifted her chin until she stared up at him. Her mouth was dry. She swallowed. "Abortion?"

His smile was sharp, cruel. "Think I didn't know?"

Kate's hand groped for a chair. She found one near the narrow kitchen doorway and fell into it. Francesca. Francesca and her myriad of lies. How could she make up such a nasty story? "How could she?"

A bark of hard laughter shot her attention to Mack. "Finally discovering that your sister can't hold her tongue?"

Had she spoken those words aloud? She blinked. "What did Robert say?"

Mack's voice was bitter. "He ranted. I got the impression that he blames me."

"For what?"

"Weren't you listening?" Mack demanded. "Forcing you into this abortion." He rubbed a hand over his jaw, his eyes, ran fingers through his hair. "But Francesca told me the truth."

"And what was that?"

"Here's the innocent act again," Mack blew out a hot breath. "All right." He dragged a chair over the tiles and sat across it. "You asked." His dark eyes gleamed and Kate prayed it wasn't hatred sparking in their depths.

"You told her that we're divorcing." His jaw tightened briefly. "It seems keeping anything to yourself is something neither of you can do. So, divorcing? And the fact that I know the baby isn't mine means you're worried about the settlement."

Kate blinked. How could an abortion solve that? "It doesn't make sense."

Mack shook his head. "I've always known money drove you. But this is low, even for you."

"What?"

"Damn it, Kate. I *know* you plan to abort this baby if I don't stump up some serious cash." He focused on her abdomen and there was something bleak in his expression. "I couldn't live with that on my conscience."

She was wrong. Francesca had sunk to depths she couldn't even begin to imagine. "And you believe her?"

Mack sighed and his whole body seemed to sag. Lines etched his forehead. The spark had gone from his eyes. "I didn't want to. I wanted to believe you could change, that you could..." He climbed to his feet, his sentence unfinished. "But you had to slap me in the face with this." He straightened and the man Kate knew was back. Hard. Untouchable.

Anything they had together was gone, but she couldn't leave him knowing that he thought her capable of something so horrible. "None of it's true, Mack," she said. "None of it."

"Discussion's over. I'll give you whatever sum you want. You win, Kate."

She was on her feet. "No. I don't want your money."

"You're going through with it." Dark eyes narrowed on her. "Don't you think Thorpe should have a say in what happens to his baby?"

Kate expelled a heated breath. "I told you. Robert's my friend. Nothing more." She tugged on his hand, pressing it to her belly. "This baby is yours."

Mack pulled his hand away, as if touching the new life growing inside her was distasteful. "There's no need to keep up this pretense."

"You've always doubted me."

He gripped her arms and Kate held back a wince. Muscles were still sore from the Colonel's bony hands. "I expect more and yet you always manage to disappoint," he muttered. "Look at the way you've treated Francesca."

Kate stared. That was too much. He would not defend Francesca to her, not after what she had said. "I've given her every penny I own, every penny I've made. Why do you think I'm broke, Mack? Your mistress bled me dry."

"Mistress." The word was too quiet.

"Oh, don't deny it. As you can't deny Anthea. Angela." She was becoming reckless. She couldn't continue, it was too dangerous. For Mack to even suspect that she was jealous, hurt by his affairs. And where that suspicion would take him. He didn't want her love. He couldn't know. He loved Francesca. Not her. "Let me go, Mack. We'll both make more sense in the morning."

His hands released her. "Angela was a mistake."

Kate stopped. Her heart pounded at the softly spoken confession. "A mistake?"

"I'd just thrown you out. I was drunk. Angela had split with her boyfriend. Found out that he was already engaged. Two people who needed solace." He sighed. "It's no excuse." His eyes held hers. "I didn't know you knew, that you saw."

A part of Kate crumbled. Angela Craven hadn't been a part of his life when he was married to her. The thought had been a spike through her heart for years. Finally, to be free of it. But did that mean he had cared for her, loved her in the short few months of marriage? She closed her eyes. How could that hurt more?

"Thank you."

"For what?"

"Telling me." Her slow feet took her along the rest of the darkening hallway. With his admission, she had lost something precious. For that short time, he had been hers. Hers alone.

She slipped her hand over the smooth banister. Gripped it. Mack still watched her. His stillness was unnerving. Uncertain, she met his dark, unreadable gaze. Her heart clenched. He deserved better than Francesca's mercenary affection. The loyalty to her sister, the core of her life, evaporated. Francesca herself had destroyed it.

"There is no abortion, Mack. Francesca lied."

A brown eyebrow rose. "You mean she was exaggerating again?"

Kate fought the urge to say yes. Francesca had to learn that she had to stop spreading malicious rumors to further her own ends. Mack had to know the truth. He could then make his own decision about their future.

"No." She held his gaze. "She lied."

"Are you trying to blame her now?"

Kate wanted to throw up her hands and carry on climbing the stairs. But she had to stop Francesca. If Mack…loved…her enough, maybe he would succeed with Francesca where she had failed. "I've been supporting her since I was seventeen. I promised my mother I would." She saw the disbelief in his eyes and a wry smile tugged at her mouth. "I do have the bank statements to prove it."

Mack shook his head. "She got the leftovers from your own wild spending."

Kate scrubbed at her face and held back a sigh. "She told me that you've been together for five years, that you give her a generous allowance." She sucked in a sour breath. The knowledge still hurt. So long together... Kate plowed on. "She's been taking money from both of us. I didn't...I didn't know about you and her."

Mack was staring. "Together?"

Kate smiled and weariness dragged at her face, at her body. "She told me at the dinner party. I wish I'd known earlier."

"Together?"

"Yes, Mack. Together. I realize marriage to me," she waved vaguely at her abdomen, "was forced, that you'd already proposed to Francesca."

"I'd *what?*"

Kate flinched at the anger in his voice. Was that supposed to be another of their secrets? "Mack—"

"Francesca told you that I proposed?"

Kate sighed. Her attempt to help had obviously backfired. "Look, sorry, it's none of my business. Just forget—"

"No." Mack stared up at her. "She said we were in a relationship?"

Kate made a smile pull at her mouth, felt as if she were hauling it up from her heels. "That's the one thing I believed in all of her lies."

Mack's mouth thinned. "My philandering ways again?"

"No. The way you look at her." Kate wanted to bite back those words. "I don't think—"

"Kate, we can't have this conversation with you halfway up the stairs."

She wanted to say that she didn't want this conversation at all, but stopped herself. She had to be careful. When she was tired, her tongue tended to run away. Her gaze slid over Mack standing at the bottom of the staircase. She saw whitened knuckles gripping the newel post, the set of his jaw. And he was angry. Implacable.

Her heart sank. She was about to have all of her illusions stripped away and hear him explain his close relationship with Francesca. How much he loved her.

Reluctant feet padded down the carpeted stairs and she led the way back into the kitchen.

Mack splashed water into the kettle. What was going on?

Francesca had waylaid him in the corridor outside his mother's room.

"Still learning to shave, Mack?" Her fingers hovered over the cuts across his jaw.

He was already walking. Kate could be out. Possibly know the results. His pace increased. "Just being a bit too quick," he said.

"Kate's back in that Medical area."

"Medical Assessment?" He stopped, stared at Francesca. "Did she say? Has anyone told her yet?"

"There was never anything wrong with her."

"Francesca?"

"She said she plans to have an abortion."

There were other words, vaguely heard, vaguely understood. But Mack felt only the painful contractions of his chest, his blood turned to sludge in his veins. She couldn't. How could he love her? A woman willing to sell him a baby he thought was his, but now that she believed her divorce settlement in doubt she could do that? It was a worse betrayal than the first time.

No. The baby was his. *He ignored the brief flare of pain that he wasn't the biological father. That didn't matter. The old, familiar fire burned through his gut. Kate could have her precious cash and then he would throw her out of both of their lives.*

Somewhere along the march to Medical Assessment, Francesca had melted away. And Kate was smiling at him. She looked pale, fragile. Tears glimmered and stupidly, stupidly he wanted to hold her. He concentrated on old fury. "I heard you're fine."

She blinked and a tear loosened and ran, unchecked, down her cheek. She seemed to shrivel and Mack ignored the wash of guilt.

"Yes." Her blue eyes dropped away. "I'm fine."

Mack leaned against the sink, remembered to breathe past the anger. "Tea?" He turned when his question was met with silence. Kate sat, staring at the sand-scrubbed table, shoulders hunched. Tiredness etched heavy lines in her face. "Kate?"

"Tea. All right."

Mack sat opposite, elbows resting on the table. Where to begin? Francesca had to be exaggerating. She did it all the time. It was a part of her energetic nature. But she'd never lied to him before. Doubt crept in, hollowed his stomach. Had she? "You have to have misunderstood her." He tried to keep his voice calm, reasonable. Work out the truth and let her sleep. "She always—"

"No!" Her hand tightened and knuckles stood out white against her skin. "She lied about the abortion, about the baby being Robert's."

Mack watched her take a slow, easing breath. Something he never wanted to acknowledge began to surface. Kate was honest. Had never lied to save her own skin, would never lie to hurt anyone else. A pain he didn't know he was holding faded. She was keeping his baby. Their baby. Mack closed his eyes. He was an idiot.

"I know you don't believe me, Mack. But if you…you and Francesca are to have any sort of future, she needs to know that this isn't right." Kate bit at her lip, amazed at herself. The words had rushed out before she lost the courage to say them. Mack deserved this chance…

The kettle steamed and switched off. Kate moved. She wanted something to do in the face of Mack's sudden silence. Her movements were automatic, unthinking. She poured water over the white teapot and dropped in teabags. Cups. She needed cups.

"I've been a fool."

Kate paused. "No." A smile tugged at her mouth. "Francesca fooled me a lot longer than you." She pulled two mugs off a wooden rack and poured milk into a jug. "Perhaps I shouldn't have pandered to her."

"How much of the settlement did you spend on Francesca?"

Kate stared. Absent fingers closed over the cutlery drawer and the teaspoon grew hot in her tight grip. "I didn't." She swallowed as she met his dark gleaming gaze.

"Kate you don't have to protect her now. Francesca would hardly let that much money slip by her."

"No, I mean, I didn't." She stirred the pot, trying to get her rapidly beating heart under control. She had thought the subject closed. That she wouldn't have to discuss any more of his relationship with her sister. But she had started this. "I…I never cashed that check. I sent it back."

"Kate."

Something in his tone irked her already taut nerves. "You'd agreed to pay for Francesca's school fees. That's all I took from you." Her voice dropped. "How could I take anything more? After what you said." Her eyes met his and she hid her feelings behind more words. "I had my pride."

Her hand trembled as she lifted the heavy pot, trembled further when Mack's strong fingers covered hers.

"You'll scald us both." He expelled a slow breath. "The check was cashed a week after I made it out. Put into an account you hold."

"What?" Kate stared. "I never…" The amount given had been over generous, meant to keep her silent about his folly in marrying her. How could someone— Her stomach dropped. "Oh my God. Francesca."

"And your rings?" Mack's voice was bitter.

Kate's eyes flashed to her left hand, found her finger bare. Yes. She had slammed the rings onto this very table that morning. "You took them. Francesca said a courier—" Another smash of reality. Her gaze found his. "What did she do, say?"

Mack's smile was twisted. "Gave me a ticket for a pawn shop."

"What did I do?" she murmured. "I know Mum spoiled her. Was I stupid to continue?"

"She was a grown woman when she came to me." He stood. Tension was a tight fist in his stomach. He had believed Francesca because he wanted to think the worst of Kate, because she had broken his heart. He rubbed at aching muscles in the back of his neck. "Straight out of the school I'd paid for. Said you'd blown everything, that you refused to help her."

His words trailed away. It hit him. He realized just how deep Francesca's lies went. "Kate." He heard the tremor in his own voice.

"She brought me a recording. You and your friends laughing, joking about our marriage."

"All the money I could roll in?" Her fingers closed around the hot mug. "A stupid joke, Mack." She sighed. "I'd given her a new gadget that morning, a 'must have' recordable diary. She obviously put it to good use."

Mack needed air. Francesca had been his friend. "I have to…"

Kate watched him escape from the kitchen. Was she being vindictive, exposing Francesca in this way? Mack loved her. Had seemed happy in his ignorance… And to have a loved one cruelly revealed. Kate sipped at her tea, welcoming the scalding heat of the liquid down her throat. "Yeah. Know how that feels," she murmured.

Mack stared into the darkness of the garden. Kate had been a burning irritation in his gut. He'd hated her. Hated her for using him, for wanting his money. Breaking his heart. And he'd loathed her because he couldn't replace her. No other woman had ever reached his soul.

He grimaced against his own melodrama, closed his eyes and let the cool September breeze wash over him. It galled him to be taken for such a fool. Francesca had fed him lies and he had swallowed them whole. "Idiot," he muttered. "And now it's too late."

He stared back into the house, to the golden glow of the little kitchen. He saw the shine of Kate's black hair caught over her shoulder. The sliver of creamy white skin exposed to the light. His heart thudded.

He loved her. Always had. Always would. And Kate. He didn't know how she felt. But there had to be something there. A sharp smile tugged at his mouth. They couldn't set each other on fire without it. Mack scratched at his hair. Damn it, he would make this whole mess right, even if it killed him.

Kate glanced up from her mug as Mack strode back into the kitchen. Her heart sank. There was a firm look of purpose on his hard, handsome face. He'd obviously decided to forgive Francesca.

"What do you want from me, Kate?"

Still the same old bone. His money. "I told you, I don't want anything."

"So you want Francesca and I to live happily ever after?"

Kate's heart burned and fell to ash. He had chosen Francesca. She should be happy for him, happy that he could forgive the woman he truly loved. But it only sharpened the fact that he had never loved her enough. She forced a bright smile. "Yes," she said.

She held his dark, shining eyes too briefly before she looked down to her mug. That had to be the hardest— Fingertips caressed her neck and she jumped. "Mack, please don't." The words slipped from her lips, almost lost in a sigh. "You shouldn't."

His lips brushed warm over her skin. Kate was boneless at his touch. His gentle hands lifted her from her chair. She had to tell him no. Falling to this…lust…wasn't right. For any of them. "Mack."

"You'd leave me in the clutches of that harridan?" His voice slid as warm honey over her skin, chasing away all thought. "Won't fight for me?"

His mouth covered hers. There was no burst of ruthless passion. No. This was a much more subtle attack. He savored her lips, a slow caress flowing through her with lazy heat. Kate's eyelids drifted down, letting her float on the pleasure the kiss evoked. The rich, addictive taste of Mack. Damn him. He manipulated her with such ease and she hated him for it. And herself. But she couldn't stop.

Kate clutched at his shirt, pressing herself against Mack's hard body. She nipped at his lower lip, wanting to deepen the contact. She sighed when his fingers threaded through her long hair, pulling her closer, opening his mouth and finding her tongue—

His words. Kate stared up at him. Fight? "But you love her."

His hand delayed on her jaw, a thumb brushing over moist lips. "I love you."

Time, the world, her heart, everything stopped. She had to have misheard. "What?" The word was almost strangled.

Mack smiled, but Kate saw it fade. His eyes were guarded. "I should have trusted you, but I saw my family history repeating itself. Me being married for money." The smile returned to his mouth, but it was bleak, desolate. "I loved you so much that the proof of that...broke...me."

Kate's chest ached. It was too incredible. For Mack to *love* her.

"Forgive me."

She fought the urge to burst into tears. She had to turn away and control the wild rush of emotion that swamped her. Her trembling hand gripped her mouth and she took deep, cleansing breaths.

"Kate?"

She couldn't look at him and heard him scrape a chair over the tiles, heard the creak of old wood as he sat. There was a sigh. Kate forced herself to turn. Mack had buried his face in his hand. He looked almost beaten.

She reached out to touch the coolness of his thick hair. A gentle caress. But her heart swelled. She had never, never been this happy. All pain, all doubt washed away. Mack was hers. But then a sharp prick of conscience. "What about Francesca?" she murmured. "You've been with her for five years."

"Kate." Her name was a sigh. Mack straightened, scrubbed at his face. "More of her lies. I never wanted…" His fingers slipped into hers. They felt strong and warm. "I love *you*. I know now I'll never love anyone else."

Kate choked. "Oh God, Mack." Tears did fall then.

"And I know this isn't what you want to hear. But I had to tell you. I had to try."

"Not what I wanted to hear?" Her laugh was strained. "I loved you from the minute I met you." Her hand brushed his cheek, feeling the start of new stubble. She smiled, ignoring the tightness of her skin, the wet, salty taste of her tears running to her lips. Her smile widened to a grin when she caught the disbelief in Mack's eyes. "Just one of so, so many…" Mack laughed, a free sound that caught at her heart, and pulled her close.

He rested his head against the softness of her breasts, breathing in her unique scent. The hint of vanilla and something just… Kate. Mack sighed when her slender fingers slid through his hair, began a slow, sensuous caress of his jaw, throat, neck. "You're the only woman in my life, Kate."

He felt her smile against his hair. "Perhaps not the only one."

He brushed his fingers over her abdomen and she shivered. "A little girl?" He looked up. "One of many?"

Kate's returning smile was sharp. "Don't push your luck, mister."

Mack grinned. An eyebrow rose. "How far can I push?"

His tone brought unexpected heat to Kate's cheeks. Her pulse jumped. The desire in his deep brown eyes made her legs run to water. He loved her. He *loved* her. She laughed. "You're incorrigible, Mack."

He stood, his fingers firm in hers. "Just one more thing." He led her into the hallway and searched through the jacket thrown over a stool. "Never take these off again," he muttered, his voice hard.

Kate watched him slip on the white-gold wedding band. She had missed its comforting weight. The engagement ring followed. Mack's own fingers trembled. She stared up into his dark eyes and found them a little too bright.

Kate smiled and felt her heart there. But she had to ask the question. This was all still too new. "Are you sure?"

Mack's eyes narrowed. "Do you love me?"

"Yes."

"Then I'm sure." His grin was wicked. He tugged her forward and met little resistance. "We've wasted seven years. I don't intend to waste a second longer." His eyes fixed on her. "And I'm going to make you take back the comment about me being a 'mediocre' comedian."

"No—" She squealed and broke away from his tickling fingers.

Laughing, Kate ran for the stairs, Mack close on her heels.

Never to love anyone else?

He could live with that.

Epilogue

"How did the meeting go?"

Mack loosened the knot on his tie, yanking it free from his neck. "He did it deliberately."

"Well, we knew that." Kate picked up her seven-month-old daughter from the colorful play mat. Her movements were jerky, restless. "Time for your nap, Elisabeth."

"His solicitors hounded him for a will." Mack shrugged and followed Kate out of the winter-bright room to a little side room where Elisabeth's day cot stood. He pulled over the curtains, sinking the sunny room into darkness.

"What happens now?" Kate's voice was a whisper as she laid her baby in the wooden cot. Colonel Greville Mackenzie had died a fortnight before. Alone. And largely unlamented.

"I sorted out a deal for the House and Estate staff. It was the least I could do." His mouth thinned and anger burnt in his dark eyes. "The Colonel told his solicitors that I wasn't his grandson. If I wanted to inherit I'd have to argue, to prove that I *was* related." His smile was bitter. "So the whole lot is going to the Treasury." He shrugged. "I never wanted the Northumberland estate. I don't think the Colonel ever realized."

He smiled, watching his daughter chew at a chubby fist. His anger had faded. "He obviously thought this would be the final insult."

Kate's fingers delayed on Elisabeth's silk-smooth cheek. The baby's eyes were heavy, thick dark lashes already closing over deep brown eyes. She tucked the top sheet under her arms. Reluctantly, she tore her gaze away from her daughter. "And Robert?"

Mack's eyes narrowed. "Yes. I met him for lunch."

Kate brushed gentle fingers over Elisabeth's soft, white-blonde hair, then forced herself to step away. Touching their daughter seemed to be addictive. "Did he apologize again?"

Mack gave her a wry smile. "For depriving me of yet *another* inheritance?"

"Funny, Mack." Kate turned from the room, leaving the door ajar. "Robert's never liked the idea of taking what he sees as rightfully belonging to you."

"He's too decent for his own good."

Kate glared at him.

"Joking, Kate."

His hands snaked around her waist, drawing her into the hardness of his body. Warm lips found the exposed skin of her neck and Kate shivered. She wondered whether she would ever get used to the thrill of his touch.

"He has some news."

Kate heard the uncertainty in his tone and she lifted her gaze to meet his serious eyes. She knew. Instinctively. "Francesca."

"For the past two months," Mack said.

Kate sighed. "He loves her. I suppose it was inevitable."

"He says that she says that she wants to make amends."

Kate smiled as she knew Mack intended her to. But her heart had turned away from her sister. Some things couldn't be forgiven so easily. "We'll see," she said.

"Francesca loves him too, Kate." His smile was sharp. "Perhaps the only person, other than herself. The thought of losing him." He shrugged.

"Self-reflection? Francesca?" Kate said. "I doubt it." She stroked his jaw, catching on a day's worth of stubble. "But how can you be this magnanimous?"

"I can afford to be generous." His hand captured hers and pressed her fingers to his lips. "I have more than I ever dreamed. I have a beautiful daughter." Love shone in his dark eyes. "And I have you."

Kate swallowed against the lump in her throat.

"I know what's it's like to lose your soul mate. How that can hurt." He sighed. "And if Francesca realizes only a fraction of the pain—"

Kate hugged herself to him, wanting to banish the memory of their years apart. "Have I said how much I love you today?"

"You could show me?"

She glared at him. "So that's what you're after."

Mack laughed. "I promised not to waste a second of the time we have, Kate."

He brushed the loose hair back from her face, deliberately stroking her so-sensitive skin below her ear. Kate's eyes drifted shut and she sighed. He held her, welcoming her arms around his body, and his cheek rested against the softness of her hair. He dropped a kiss there. "But this is nice too."

"I never believed that you could be such an old romantic, Mack."

"*Old?*" he demanded.

Kate grinned up at him. "—Ish."

"You do realize this conversation will have consequences."

There was a soft cry from Elisabeth's room and Kate broke away. Her blue-violet eyes were wicked. "Promise?"

He watched her disappear behind the door, her soothing voice calming their daughter.

They had been apart so long. Sometimes, when he woke up and she was in his arms, warm and soft and real, not some long wished for dream, he had to pinch himself. Mack smiled. His heart belonged to her.

He stared at the ring on his finger, rubbing his thumb against the warm gold. Almost nine years since he had first fallen for her. But they had come through the lies, the pain. Yes. A love proven through time.

Mack winced against his own slushy thoughts but then Kate appeared. He watched the winter sunlight play over her shining, black hair, making her pale skin glow. And her eyes. That amazing blue-violet held a love solely for him.

Slushy?

If it meant having Kate in his life everyday?

He could live with that too.

About the Author

Kim Rees started writing when she was ten years old. That's…okay we'll not go into how long ago that was now. But in 2002, she gave in and started writing romance…well…sex. To her surprise, it came naturally. Yes. Please groan at the pun.

Kim lives halfway between Strawberry Fields and Penny Lane. Honest. Just *please* don't ask her to sing.

To learn more about Kim Rees, please visit http://www.romancefiction.co.uk/. Join her Yahoo! group to join in the fun with other readers as well as Kim! http://groups.yahoo.com/group/daughters_of_circe/

Vengeance is what she sought…eternal love is what she found.

Fallon's Revenge
© *2006 Mackenzie McKade*

Young and inexperienced, Fallon McGregor is an immortal with one thing on her mind. Revenge. She'll do anything to destroy the demon that killed her daughter and made Fallon his flesh and blood slave. One step ahead of her tormentor, she knows her luck is running out. She needs to discover the mysteries of the dark—and fast. When she meets Adrian Trask she gets more than she bargains for in tight jeans and a Stetson.

Adrian will share his ancient blood and knowledge with Fallon, but he wants something in return…her heart and her promise to stay with him forever.

But Fallon doesn't have forever. Once her nemesis is destroyed she will seek her own death. Tormented, she must choose between a promise made and the love of one man.

Warning, this title contains the following: explicit sex, graphic language, and violence.

Available now in ebook and print from Samhain Publishing.

What he offered her was not a wise decision. His blood was powerful. He shared it sparingly and never without justifiable cause. The exchange—and there would be an exchange, he couldn't wait to taste her—would form a blood bond for all time. The link between them would be a tracking mechanism and open up a special mental path between them and through her, possibly, her Master.

Without warning his fangs burst past his gums, the taste of blood in his mouth. He tipped his head and let it flow to the back of his throat, awakening his beast with a roar. Dark and dangerous, it sought out the animal which lay within her.

The feminine reply was sexy as it wrapped around him. He sensed it moving just below her pale skin, teasing and taunting him.

Adrian thought he felt a drop of moisture on his hand. He glanced skyward. Heavy clouds had gathered threatening rain, as they moved into the shadows.

"Where are you taking me?" Her voice was low and throaty, a hint of arousal, but no fear apparent in her question.

And there should have been.

Even in the crowded bar he could have cast a spell to render them invisible or even planted suggestions in the minds of the humans to mask what they saw. For some unknown reason he wanted her to himself, alone. The need to mark her was becoming an obsession and all out crazy because she belonged to another.

He ignored her question and instead he asked, "What is your name, darlin'?"

She cocked her head with a haughty tilt. "Does it matter? You're just a fly-by-night snack for me before I'm on my way."

Rich laughter rolled from his lips. She was going to hold onto her hard-ass act to the bitter end. "A snack? Me?" She had some nerve.

With preternatural speed he pulled her into his arms and they vanished from the wooded area.

When the world stopped churning around him he held her close, his lips a breath away from hers as they stood in the middle of his bedroom. A fire burned in the flagstone fireplace, radiating warmth upon his back. "I plan to make a four-course meal out of you," he murmured, his mouth moving across hers as he spoke. And then he kissed her.

He sipped lightly from her mouth, gliding his tongue along the seams of her full lips. His arms tightened around her as he slanted his head and pressed harder, wanting and needing to get closer. She was soft and pliable beneath his assault. He nipped at her bottom lip and her mouth parted to allow him in.

As his tongue thrust between her lips, her incisors pushed through gum and bone releasing a swirl of blood. Raw hunger sounded, forcing a low timbre from his throat. She tasted of the sweetest honey as he stroked the roof of her mouth and caressed the length of her fangs.

There was nothing sexier than an aroused vampiress. Her taste was an aphrodisiac. Her sensuality could not be compared to that of a mere human. And this particular woman shimmered with sex appeal, an energy Adrian swore wrapped him tightly around her little finger.

But he would never show his hand—at least not yet.

The female whimper that echoed in his mouth stirred his lust like no one had ever done before. Their bodies parted. Both of them were breathing hard, lust burning bright as they stared into each other's eyes.

"Fallon." Her tongue skimmed across her swollen lips as if capturing the last of his kiss. "My name is Fallon McGregor."

Adrian studied her flushed face. She was beautiful.

"Adrian Trask," he shared before taking her mouth once again, because he couldn't stop himself.

Dammit. He couldn't get enough of her. He drank greedily. His fingers played with the knot of leather at her back holding her halter top in place. He needed to see her naked, feel her body beneath his.

She pulled away from him, breaking the kiss. "Whoa, cowboy."

But it was too late. The knot came free in Adrian's hand and the scrap of material floated down her sides, coming to rest between two plump and perky breasts.

Her eyes widened in surprise. Rosy nipples grew into hard pebbles, before his heated stare.

"Remove it," he demanded, unable to take his sight from her beauty.

"But—"

He didn't wait for her denial. "I want you naked, beneath me as you take my blood into your veins and my cock into your body."

"But—"

With a need to see her naked, he willed the material to disappear with a simple thought. The halter top dissolved before his eyes.

She was a tiny thing, but full of attitude.

With a toss of her head she sent her hair over her shoulders, baring her further. A small, tucked waist and curves made to be stroked enticed him. But it was her breasts, which would fit perfect in his palms, that called to him.

"I don't remember sex being in the deal, cowboy." Her voice was a soft rasp that stirred his blood. "Just a small bite, then I leave—remember?"

No way could she just walk out of his life. Where that thought came from he didn't know. All he knew was for the night, she was his.

"Darlin', I can't let you leave until I've had a taste of you. All of you." He waited a heartbeat for her refusal, a refusal that never came.

Instead, she purred, "Make it quick, lover-boy. I'm on a schedule."

Her futile attempt to appear unmoved by his touch failed miserably when he cupped her breast. She gasped, and he felt the tremor that assailed her. Her eyes darkened. With his heightened sense of smell he breathed in the flood of pheromones she released in response.

Featherlight, his thumb brushed across her taut nipple, back and forth, again and again. "Anything worth doing right should be done nice and…" his other hand pushed beneath her hair and grasped the nape of her neck, "…slow." He drew her head back, baring her throat.

The vein beneath her skin bulged, begging to be taken. Gently, he drew her closer, dipped his head, and ran his tongue over the vessel carrying life to her heart. It pulsed beneath his pursuit, fast little beats which gave her arousal away.

She wanted him.

"Do it," she groaned, her hips brushed against his swollen groin. "Take me, now."

Discover the Talons Series

5 STEAMY NEW PARANORMAL ROMANCES TO HOOK YOU IN

Kiss Me Deadly, by Shannon Stacey
King of Prey, by Mandy M. Roth
Firebird, by Jaycee Clark
Caged Desire, by Sydney Somers
Seize the Hunter, by Michelle M. Pillow

AVAILABLE IN EBOOK—COMING SOON IN PRINT!

WWW.SAMHAINPUBLISHING.COM